EDEN
UNTOUCHED

Patricia Alexander LeBeauf

ISBN 978-1-0980-3048-3 (paperback)
ISBN 978-1-0980-4847-1 (hardcover)
ISBN 978-1-0980-3049-0 (digital)

Christian Faith Publishing, Inc.
832 Park Avenue
Meadville, PA 16335
www.christianfaithpublishing.com

Printed in the United States of America

Acknowledgments

First of all, I give all glory and honor to God for without Him being in my life, this book would not have been possible. It is He who have given me my talents and gifts, and I hope you enjoy reading my book as much as I have enjoyed writing it.

To be honest, there were days that I was too afraid to work on it because I was afraid that the ideas wouldn't come.

That's when I had to put my trust in God and to know that "fear" wasn't from Him.

My sons, Demondre' Edwards, his wife Margit, David, his girl-friend Christine, Alexander, his wife Candice and Robere', and his wife Vanessa, who kept telling me that I can do this and not to give up, and through my grandkids who didn't even know that they have been a constant source of inspiration as I see life through their creative minds when we play together—making up stories, watching them put puzzles together, or even just watching them try to imitate sounds coming from their parents. It's the small things that they do that amazes me.

To my family and many friends, who I called personally instead of texting, to let you know that I was having my book published. You encouraged me by often asking me how you could pray for me and also how was the process going for the publication my book?

My prayer partners, Veronica Fair, and Sharon. We have been praying together once a week for over 15 years and on the phone on Monday nights for over the last 7 years when one of us moved to Kansas, we did not let that interfere with what God has started. You two have been on this journey with me from the beginning and kept me lifted up with both scriptures and encouraging words to let me know that I can do this!

Pastor Kenny Briscoe. When I first shared with you about my idea for my book, I'll never forget your simple advice that you gave me, "let your imagination run wild!"

Pastor Don Roy. My friend, my shepherd, in whom I received a solid foundation for my walk with God, who helped me with my book to ensure that my writing was biblically correct. Thank you and Pastor Viki for believing in me, nurturing and encouraging me to speak in front of crowds, allowing me to create skits that were performed at your church. You two saw something in me that I didn't even know was there.

To my mama. Clemmie Ruth, who never stopped believing in me, who knew from my earliest childhood days that God had given me a creative mind and talent to write.

My husband Valentino. My "Tino." To see the pride and excitement in your eyes for me when I shared my exciting news about my book being accepted by a publishing company was worth the time and effort I put forth to create this book. I'm so glad that you're on this exciting journey with me.

Jedidiah Jamison

J edi thought to himself, *How could this have happened to me again? So many times in the last three years, even I have lost count. Should I keep driving?* he thought. *Do I go to the twin's apartment or go home to face the music?* At this moment he felt a sense of peace that he knew that everything was going to be all right, no matter how dreary it looked at the moment.

So he turned his car around and headed in the direction of his home.

Jedi was your average person who felt that no one had any high expectations for him.

He was the third of five children and had that middle child syndrome. At the age of twenty-seven, he still felt that he wasn't loved as much as his siblings since he wasn't the firstborn or even the baby of the family. This had an effect on him growing up.

Growing up being biracial didn't help Jedi. Even though prejudice was not in the world, he felt that he didn't belong to one specific race or another. This was something no one talked about because it was just accepted as a part of life.

On this particular day, Jedi quietly tried to enter the house without his mom hearing him come in. It was the middle of the day, and there will be questions as to why he was home at this hour.

In the family room, his mom Ruth was going over the internet to see who might be hiring teachers. Her "mom ears" perked up as she leaned toward the front door to see who was entering, since all of her five children with the exception of Jedi had moved out, and it was too early for anyone to be home. She called out, "Who's there?"

Jedi then comes in hanging his head.

Ruth looks up from her laptop into the eyes of her child that looks exactly like her, but a much lighter version, and knows immediately that something is wrong.

Jedi starts to explain to his mom before she can even open her mouth. "Mom, this time it really wasn't my fault!" How many times in the past three years had Ruth heard this excuse every time Jedi ended up getting fired from his job? Ruth thinks to herself, *My child, my child.*

Ruth and her husband Felix have been married, going on thirty-one years. They met when they were attending the same college.

Felix was a good-looking tall white boy with hazel eyes that can look into your soul and would make you want to tell him everything, if you're not careful. The fact that Felix's major was in history and his minor in genealogy was unusual because he didn't look like your typical nerd. If you had to guess his major solely on his looks, you would guess his major was drama or that he was a jock.

Ruth was the exact opposite of Felix. She was of African descent with a dark chocolate creamy complexion, tall like Felix, and walked with her head held high as if she was royalty.

Felix was intrigued by Ruth the very first time he saw her on campus and made it his sole mission to get to know her better.

Ruth's major was in teaching, and she was a no-nonsense person. She had two goals, and they were first to graduate and then second, to become a teacher.

After weeks, which turned into months of pursuing Ruth, she finally, reluctantly, went on a date with Felix. She thought to herself *that after just one date, maybe he will leave me alone.*

Was she ever wrong! During that first date, they did nothing but talk. They had so much in common and fell deeply in love before the date had ended.

They both decided they would get married as soon as they graduated and found stable jobs.

Now Felix had been interning as a historian with a company whose main responsibility was to keep track of everything that had happened since the beginning of time, and they also had a genetic lab on site where they conducted research on the different ethnicities around the world.

As interracial marriages were beginning to be more prevalent, this company kept track of the different lineages throughout the world and would be able to tell from the DNA the reversal path a family's trait took from present time back to Adam and Eve.

Yes, back to Adam and Eve.

Since Felix had been interning during the summers of both his junior and senior years, the company was so impressed with his knowledge and aptitude for both history and genetics and how he completed his assignments with accuracy and speed, they decided to offer him a full-time position on staff once he graduated.

This meant that he and Ruth could get married as soon as they both graduated.

Ruth became pregnant right away, and both decided that it would be best if she stayed at home to raise the baby. Their first baby was a boy, and they named him Shiloh, which means "one who belongs." His complexion was that of his mom's, but he looked exactly like his dad—hazel eyes with a clump of blonde hair.

Two years later, along came Rebekah, and one year after that, Jedidiah, who they nicknamed Jedi because his name was too long for such a little boy.

Five years and two kids later, Ruth and Felix found themselves pregnant again. This time with twins, one boy and one girl.

Felix was the one with a sense of humor in the family and didn't want to give them names that were from The Book and decided that he wanted to name his daughter Ebony and his son Ivorie. The sense of humor was that Ebony was the one with the light complexion, while Ivorie had the darker complexion.

As the Jamison family settled into family routines, the personalities of each child became apparent to the parents with the exception of Jedi.

He blended in the background which broke his mom's heart because she knew even though all of her kids were exceptionally smart, Jedi was the smartest one of them all.

"What happened this time, Jedi?" His mom asked.

"Well, like I said before, Mom," Jedi began, "this time it wasn't my fault. I have been coming to this place for over a year, have been always on time, and have never missed a day, so you would have thought that they would have given me a little slack for this one mistake."

In the back of Ruth's mind, she had already begun to formulate the scenario of why Jedidiah was fired.

Jedi had worked at an assembly plant for televisions. These televisions were the top of the line. Not only was it just a television, it had the capability to be linked to your telephone with automatic FaceTime. That's right, if you had an incoming call while you were watching television, you can put your program on pause, click on the incoming call, and voila! You're now not only speaking with the person but seeing them at the same time on the television.

Of course, your television is equipped with caller ID so if you didn't want to answer the call, you could personalize the voice message for the person who was calling you. How exciting is that?

If it's your mom, you could say something like "Hey Mom, I'm so sorry that I'm not able to take your call right now, and I'm really looking forward to spending next weekend with you and Dad. I'll call you back as soon as I can, and Mom, don't forget that I love you from here to eternity." What mother wouldn't be ecstatic after hearing that?

Or maybe if it was that important call you were expecting regarding that interview you had for a new job and you weren't looking your best, you could tailor the voice message to say something to the effect of "Thank you very much for the opportunity to interview for the position of administrative assistant yesterday, and I am so sorry that I am not available at this moment to take your call. I enjoyed speaking with you, meeting other members of the staff, and the opportunity to learn more about the company. I am very interested in this position and the opportunity to join your team. I will call you back within the next ten minutes. Looking forward to speaking with you."

With that kind of message, the job is yours!

Well, someone forgot to tell Jedi that this specific program could be added to the television if it was paid for, so when the televisions were ready to be packed, Jedi added that specific program as part of the package, ready to be shipped to the stores.

This mistake wasn't caught until the company realized that for over a month no one was buying this specific program, and when it was recently surveyed, people all over thought it was a great idea and said that they would definitely buy it.

When they had contacted over half of the consumers who recently bought the model, they told the stores how much they enjoyed the realistic view of the television, but more than that, they enjoyed how their television was linked to their iPhones and how they could create personalized voice messages.

Well, the rest is history. It had been tracked down to Jedi's shift that this model of televisions were packaged and shipped.

The company enjoyed having Jedi work for them during this time, and he proved that he was a valued employee, but this was a costly mistake, and they sadly had to let the entire shift go.

Once Ruth heard the full story, she did side with Jedi but decided they need to come up with a plan before his father came home that day.

"Why don't you work with your dad?" Ruth suggested.

Jedi looked at his mom as if she had been staring at her computer too long and reading too many want ads, only because he didn't want to tell her exactly what he was feeling. So he continued to look at her with a blank look on his face.

"Now Jedi, before you say no," his mom continues, "just listen to what I have to say. You're a bright and intelligent young man who is still looking to find himself, and at your father's job, there might be a position available that might interest you. You'll never know until you try, and what do you have to lose? It's not as if you have some place pressing to go, and who knows, you might even find your future wife there."

At this comment about the wife, Jedi rolled his eyes and went to his room.

A few hours later, Felix came home and was greeted by his wife as she sat in the living room with a concerned look on her face. "What did our dear Jedi do now?" said Felix.

Ruth stood up to greet her husband with a hug and a kiss and said, "That's not funny, and how do you know that I'm not concerned about any of our other kids?"

"Well", said Felix, "is it?"

"No," replied Ruth, "you're right, it's about Jedi. He got fired again, and before you say anything, this time it wasn't his fault, and we also came up with a solution."

"We?" said Felix.

"Yes, we," answered Ruth, "but I think you'd better sit down to take this all in."

"That bad, huh," said Felix.

"No, silly, that great of an idea," Ruth said, who was the optimist in the family. "Have a seat and keep an open mind, babe, as I explain what we were thinking. We were thinking that Jedi could come and work with you."

Ruth braced herself to hear something negative from Felix, and when he said, "Go on," she nearly fell out of her chair.

"Well," began Ruth, "you know how you're always saying how you could use another assistant on your team to ensure history, as it is still happening throughout the world, is accurately being added in the archives and another to do the research?"

"Yes," said Felix, not sure if he liked where this conversation was heading. "I do believe I did mention that a few times or so, so what?"

"Wouldn't it be great to have Jedi help you?" Ruth rushed on to say. "We both know that recently he has been trying to find himself. and what a better place than in the archives of the history of the world? Think of it. Felix, with Jedi assisting in the research department, it will allow another experienced team member to concentrate on adding events as they are happening in the world. With that type of responsibility, think how this assignment will improve his confidence."

"He'll read about things that happened in the past that some of us didn't even know, and maybe it will get him to think about his own future."

"Since you're your own boss," continued Ruth, "you can hire and fire anyone you want to, so give him a chance babe. Anyway, how much trouble can Jedi get into just researching?"

Felix was thinking along the same lines as his wife and agreed to give Jedi a chance. A six-month probationary chance.

Jedi started working with his dad the following Monday and was excited that he didn't have to get dressed up like his dad, but more importantly, he was excited that he was to be placed in the "dungeon," the name given to the place where the history books were kept, even though they have been converted to files on computers. Some of the books that have been around since Adam and Eve were made of papyrus. It was important that the temperature in the dungeon was set at a temperature of seventy-two degrees, with a built-in humidifier that kept the air clear of dust. Thank goodness the durability of paper continued to improve in the future, along with a number of other things.

The company, since all the books have been converted to files on the computers, had been thinking of getting completely rid of the books as they were just taking up space, and Felix had been the thorn in their side, trying to convince them it would be a disaster to get rid of "history." So they gave Felix some time to present his case of why they shouldn't get rid of the books.

Jedi had been hearing about this place from his dad ever since he could remember, but never did he show the excitement that was welling up inside every time his dad talked about it. Until now.

"Well, son," his dad said, "within the walls of this dungeon, the history of our world, starting with your grandparents (without having to say how many great, great) Adam and Eve, are being carefully stored on the computers for future generations to read about. You are not the only person who has access down here, so don't feel like you are ever alone."

The other members of the team have other responsibilities, and like you, so we can keep this operation going. Your first assignment is to find out how many people have tried to gain access to the tree of knowledge. We know that we, not only as historians, but we also play an important part by putting together a plan that would prevent any future plans of anyone trying to gain access to the tree of knowledge which would upset our way of life."

"It's been told that ever since God kicked that snake of a person Lucifer out of heaven along with his buddies because he thought himself as highly as the Almighty God, he has been roaming the earth trying to convince others to take a bite from the fruit that came from the tree of knowledge like he did your grandmother Eve. The good news is that his buddies have been contained inside the garden of Eden." Felix ended with "Could you imagine what chaos they would try to bring on earth if they were allowed to roam the earth with their ringleader?"

Two Thousand Years Before

L et's talk about the history of creation, how in the beginning God created the heavens and the earth, how the earth was formed and void, and darkness surrounded the atmosphere.

As the Bible tells us, God made daylight. He separated the land from the water and called it Earth.

The Bible also goes on to tell us how God created the different types of seeds that would make fruits and vegetables and the different types of living creatures—birds in the air, sea creatures, beasts of the earth, and even creepy crawling things. God told the animals to be fruitful and multiply.

Then God said, "Let Us make man in Our image, according to Our likeness, let them have dominion over the fish of the sea, over the birds of the air, and over every creeping thing that creeps on the earth."

Our image, Our likeness? What is God saying here? That He wanted mankind to look like Him?

Well yes, but God also wanted mankind to represent Him and to have traits like Him—to have qualities such as reasoning, a strong sense of intellect, having a moral compass along with having individual personalities. The capacity to relate to others, to hear, to see, and to speak. Could you image if these senses were not part of our DNA?

As the Bible goes on to say, so God created man in His own image—in the image of God. He created him, male and female. He created them. Then God blessed them; and God said to them, "Be fruitful and multiply; fill the earth and subdue it."

What! Subdue the animals? Subdue, meaning to bring under control, suppress, overwhelm. Well, you get the picture—to have dominion over the fish of the sea, over the birds of the air, and over every living thing that moves on the earth.

The Lord God formed man out of the dust of the ground and breathed into his nostrils the breath of life, and man became a living being.

Did you know that God is a relationship God because He breathed life into man, which is very intimate? He didn't breathe life into the cattle, the sea creatures, or any of the other animals, only man.

The Lord God planted a garden eastward in Eden, and there He put the man He had formed in it. Eden means a delightful place.

Out of the ground the Lord God made every tree grow that is pleasant to the sight and good for food. In the lush natural reserves were found the two trees that are the keys to everything that follows in history. They were the physical means God used to preform spiritual realities. The tree of life is associated with experiencing the life of God including immorality. The tree of knowledge of good and evil represents human autonomy, which is self-rule and an assumed independence from God in all areas of life. Both of these trees were located in the middle of the garden.

Then the Lord God took the man and put him in the garden of Eden to tend and keep it. Otherwise *guard it!*

"Of every tree of the garden you may freely eat," commanded the Lord God, "but of the tree of knowledge of good and evil you shall not eat, for in that day that you eat of it you shall surely die."

This story will have a twist so stay with it.

When the Lord God looked around at what He had created, He said, "It is not good that man should be alone; I will make him a helper comparable to him." A helper comparable to him meant complementarity to him.

So the Lord God created every beast of the field and every bird of the air and brought them to Adam to see what he would call them.

Can you imagine God standing around with His hand under His chin, thinking, *What in the world will this man name these animals?* When Adam named the animal that we currently call pig, do you think God flinched and said, "No, that animal's name should be cow"? "He's pink like a cow and will roll in the mud like a cow."

No, God left Adam to name every animal because He gave him dominion over everything.

Adam gave names to all the cattle, to the birds of the air, and to every beast of the field, but for Adam there was not a helper found that was comparable to him. Even a dog, being man's best friend, was not complementarity to Adam.

The shift in history is about to take place. Wait for it!

And the Lord God caused a deep sleep to fall on Adam, and he slept. God is a compassionate God. He caused Adam to fall into a deep sleep because by opening Adam's side and taking out the rib would cause pain. What better type of anesthetic than a natural sleep from God. He took one of his ribs and closed up the flesh in its place. The rib, which the Lord God had taken from man, He made into a woman, and He brought her to the man.

Now being the Lord God, He could have taken a strand of Adam's hair and made a woman out of it.

Can't we determine DNA from a strand of hair? But as we said before, God enjoys having a relationship, and the rib was chosen as a representation of an intimate part of Adam's makeup. This part of Adam's body was in the middle part of his body. Not too high nor too low. This was to indicate that she was to neither control him or be controlled by him. This particular rib was close to his heart.

Adam then said, "This is now bone of my bones and flesh of my flesh; she shall be called woman because she was taken out of man." Adam named her Eve.

Not only was this woman a compliment to Adam, he recognized immediately something of himself in her. She was a part of himself, his "other self."

God instructed that they should "be joined" and "become one flesh," not to do things that are of importance without first checking with one another.

One day as Eve was walking in the garden of Eden, there was a serpent who was more cunning than any beast of the field which the Lord God had made. When he saw that Eve was alone, he said to the woman, "Has God indeed said, you shall not eat of every tree of the garden?"

The woman replied, "We may eat the fruit of the trees of the garden, but of the fruit of the tree of knowledge which is in the midst of the garden, God has said, 'You shall not eat it, nor shall you touch it, lest you die.'"

Now did all the other animals speak or just the serpent? At that moment Eve should have thought about that and kept walking or better yet, ran!

The serpent continued talking to Eve. He told her that if she ate the fruit, she will not surely die. The serpent also said, "For God knows that in the day you will eat of it, your eyes will be opened, and you will be like God, knowing good and evil."

How would Eve know what good and evil was or what was the difference between good and evil? Just a little something to make you wonder.

So when the woman saw that the tree was in fact good for food, that it was pleasant to the eyes and a tree desirable to make one wise, how could she resist?

She took the fruit, examined it very closely, started to eat it, and before she could take a bit out of the fruit, Adam came out of nowhere, saw what she was about to do, and knocked the fruit out of Eve's hand!

Yes, Eve did not eat the fruit!

Adam began questioning her, asking her, "Why would you even think about eating from that tree, knowing that God had said that we would die?"

Eve began pouting and tried to explain that the serpent told her that she could indeed eat the fruit and that they would not die and tried to get Adam to understand why she did it.

Adam gently took Eve by the arm, and as they walked through the garden, he explained what their mission was. God had given them complete dominion over all the entire earth, and with this responsibility, they had to set the example and to trust that God knew best. By the time Adam had convinced Eve what their mission was, and Eve was satisfied, she promised Adam that she wouldn't ever think of eating from that tree again. Adam wanted to confront the serpent, but the serpent had quietly disappeared.

Once this event happened to Eve, Adam knew that it would only be sometime before Satan tried again to tempt someone else with lies so they would want to eat from the tree.

God also knew about the confrontation between Eve and the serpent and was pleased that Adam intervened and stopped Eve from eating the fruit.

The serpent had left the scene, but God was not about to let this situation go unnoticed.

When He found the serpent, He said to him, "Because you tried to twist my words, confuse, and deceive the woman of the things of which I had told them not to do, you are more cursed than all cattle and every beast of the field and on your belly you shall go and you shall eat dust forever."

Now we know why a snake slithers.

The fact that the serpent was always going to be in the world, and his nature is to be deceitful, dishonest, and confusing, God placed a cherubim that sat on bed of pearls at the east side of the garden of Eden. He held a flaming sword whose handle was made also of pearls, which turned every which way he did and their purpose was to guard the entry way to the tree of knowledge.

Cherubim are the created angels being assigned to guard the throne of God.

"Cherubim" is plural for "cherub" so God had cherubim on guard 24/7 moving to His direction. Since we know that *cherubim* is another word for angels, let's just say angels.

In every group, there is a leader, and with the group of angels, there was no exception.

Michael, the archangel, was created to be both a protector and the leader of the army of God.

Michael and his co-leader Gabriel were in charge of selecting which angels would have the honor of guarding the tree of knowledge.

Michael took his job very seriously and would on occasions try to sneak in the garden just to see how well the angels responded to sneak attempts to enter the garden. Those angels that Michael and

Gabriel were able to get pass were not selected and were sent back to heaven. Those who passed the first test were given a second test—the human beings!

Michael went as far as giving creative suggestions to human beings while they slept to see if they could get pass the angels and were pleased to see how well the angels responded when the human beings tried to enter but did not succeed. These were the angels that were kept and given the high honor of guarding the tree of knowledge.

Once Michael and Gabriel had recruited the angels that would be needed for the job and had kept an eye on them for centuries, they decided that they were no longer needed to be around the tree of knowledge.

God's plan was for us populate the entire earth so when people began to get curious about what was around the corner, so to speak, they began to explore other parts of the earth.

By this time, people had horses and had also invented boats as means of transportation.

Because different parts of the earth had different climates, people's skin and facial features began changing.

God thinks of everything. For example, something as small as our eyelids. It's called the epicanthic fold which depicts it as an adaptation to the tropical and arctic regions where many Asians live.

The fold is described as a sun visor protecting the eyes from overexposure to ultraviolet radiation or as a blanket insulating them from the cold. Now even though quite a few of the races have this fold, it is more prevalent in the Asian culture.

What about the different colors of our skin? Variations in human skin color is determined in traits that depend with geography and the sun's ultraviolet radiation, what we commonly call the UV rays.

Those closer to the equator tend to have darker skin tones so that their skin could be protected from the sun, than those who chose to go to cooler climates with less sunlight developed lighter skin tones.

As groups of races settled in specific regions of the earth, some again became curious and set out, settling with other races and started intermarrying.

What a beautiful thing to happen.

During this time, God still walked around like He did with Adam and Eve, and He would have those who were called prophets write down certain things that others might not understand at this particular time but would become very useful in the future.

These were the people who would be considered more in tune with God. Let's say God had their ears, and they didn't turn away from Him. These are the prophets of God. When they heard from God, the prophets told others exactly what God had said without adding or subtracting any of His words. These words were inspirations breathed by God and would be written down in "The Book of the Law."

There was even talk among the prophets about a time in the future that didn't seem possible—a time when God would no longer walk around with the people, and people would start dying because sin had entered the world. When we say walk, it's meant figuratively; you could sense His presence like the wind. You can feel it, you can see the effects of it, but you can't see it physically.

The Book of the Law would be put away in the archives, collecting dust, and the only time words were added was by the prophets.

Jedi

"It's been told," started Felix, "that God kicked that snake of a person Lucifer out of heaven along with his buddies because he thought himself as highly as the Almighty God, and he has been known to roam the earth ever since trying to convince others to take a bite out of the fruit from the tree of knowledge like he did your grandmother Eve. The good news is that his buddies have been contained inside the garden of Eden.

"Could you imagine what chaos they would bring if they were allowed to roam the earth together with their ring leader?

"Thank goodness after your grandfather Adam knocked the fruit from your grandmother's Eve's hand before she could eat it, God placed an angel that sat on a bed of pearls east of the garden of Eden, who held a flaming sword whose handle was made also of pearls, which turned every way, and their sole purpose was to guard the entry way to the tree of knowledge."

"There's your computer, son," Felix continued, "which you now have your own login and password, and Jedi, please be careful with this computer because the company hasn't spared any expense when buying equipment that will store and maintain our history which includes the integrity of our way of life. Also I'm hoping those books might come in handy when you're doing your research because the company is trying to destroy them, so feel free to use them too.

"I'll see you around five o'clock. You'll have an hour for lunch, and there are plenty of places to eat around here, so just make sure you lock your computer every time you leave. Good luck, son, on your first day," ended Felix.

"Thanks Dad," his son replied.

Jedi couldn't wait to begin! Just breathing the same air that housed all those history books did something to him that he couldn't explain.

After logging into the computer, he put in "first break-in for the tree of knowledge" because he was interested in creating a spreadsheet from the beginning of time to the present. Jedi realized if he kept track of all the attempted break-ins, he would discover a pattern along with their errors, which would allow him to design a perfect fail-safe plan so no one would be able to enter where the tree of knowledge was kept.

The more Jedi thought about his plan, the more excited he became. "If I wanted to gain access to the tree of knowledge," Jedi repeated to himself, *Wouldn't I want to know how others failed, so I could make improvements and create the perfect plan by using the technology we have today? My parents, sisters, brothers, and all my relatives would be so proud of me. Not to mention that my name would go down in history!*

By the year 2050, man would have enclosed the tree of knowledge with security which would have improved over time because of the many attempts made by man to enter in.

The rest of the garden could still be enjoyed by the world. The tree of knowledge had two types of security—one heavenly with the angels guarding it and one made by man.

You had to first manage to get by the security made by man then by God's angels.

So he began his research with the year 1920.

D'Artagnan Greenberg, 1920

D'Artagnan Greenberg grew up in a French-Jewish home, if you couldn't tell by his name.

His friends and family called him Dar because everyone felt that the name D'Artagnan belonged to someone who was sophisticated, someone that would be doing something with his life other than drawing cartoons.

Drawing in itself was a gift, but cartoons? No one had ever seen cartoons before, so people were slow to give it a chance—especially since both his parents were prominent people.

Dar's mother's family was from the South of France and was a student of the culinary arts. Ever since Francesca could walk, she was intrigued with the different smells that had come out of her parent's kitchen, and she wanted to be a part of the process that put together such incredible aromas.

She went to Israel hoping to expand her culinary knowledge to another type of cuisine—Mediterranean food.

Dar's father Joshua and many generations prior to him were doctors of medicine. Yes, even though no one had any knowledge of anyone dying, with the exception of animals, there were people in the world who were curious about the human body and how it functioned, and of course there were always "accidents" that needed to be tended to—broken bones, stomach aches, sprains, etc., things that happened to our body that required medical attention but didn't lead to death.

As the population grew, more and more people were beginning to be curious about other things as well—sturdier structures, electricity, better modes of transportation, better ways to communicate. Of course schools were being established around the world for the purpose of higher learning in all different areas of occupations and careers, with the exception of medicine.

Since the need for doctors was not highly in demand, by the year 1920, there were only ten colleges throughout the entire world who would teach, equip, and send those who were interested in medicine to different parts of the world.

They did not have medicine to distribute but relied on the vegetation and herbs that came from the earth, which is the way God had intended it to be. For example, mint. Mint is not only good for freshening our breath, but it's also good for calming the stomach.

The lavender plant is not only beautiful to look at, but its sweet, soothing scent is perfect for helping us to relax and sleep better.

For burns, just spread on the gel from the aloe vera plant.

Ginger, we can't leave ginger out. Ginger can be used as a natural relief for when we're nausea.

What about those times when our stomach might be tied-in knots and we haven't had a bowel movement in a few days and the relief for this? Rhubarb. Who knew? In order to use rhubarb for constipation, the stalk is the part that needs to be used, not the leaves.

These are just a few of the ways our natural resources could be used in the medical society.

Because medicine was one area of an occupation that did not have a definite answer for everything, doctors started using the term "practicing medicine."

Francesca had met Dr. Greenberg when she had an accident at the restaurant where she was the sous chef and had slipped on some food in the galley. Not only did Frankie, as she liked to be called, slip on some food, she managed to take a few pots and pans down with her. What a commotion that caused in the restaurant!

How lucky was Frankie that a doctor was at the restaurant during the time of her accident and came running into the galley to see if he could be of assistance.

When Joshua gently tried to see if Frankie could stand on her own, she gave out a little whimper. He immediately found a chair for her to sit on so that he could examine her better.

After he determined that her foot was not broken but badly sprained, he suggested that she come to his office across the street from the restaurant so he could properly wrap it up.

Once all the commotion had died down, and Joshua finally had a chance to take a good look at Frankie, he couldn't believe his luck. He had been coming into the restaurant for over a year, not only because it served the best Mediterranean dishes but because he secretly had been wanting to meet Frankie.

He knew she worked at the restaurant because he noticed her walking by his office on her way to work, and he followed her with his eyes all the way to the restaurant. No way was Joshua was going to let this opportunity slip by him!

Joshua took advantage of the situation and told Frankie that the best way he could get her to his office without causing any further damage to her foot was to carry her.

Joshua isn't what you would call a muscular man, but his infatuation for Frankie gave him the strength he needed to carry her to his office if it was the last thing he would do. It also didn't hurt that Frankie was only five feet even and weighed only a hundred pounds soaking wet.

So began the courtship of Joshua and Frankie.

Joshua thought all this time that he was the one who had started the relationship between he and Frankie, so he was mildly shocked when Frankie confessed to not only knowing who he was and where he worked but made it a practice to walk by his office knowing that he would be at the window looking out.

Frankie also confessed that not only did she go out of her way by walking that same route, she made it her business to know how often and what days he would come to the restaurant to eat.

Did Frankie really have an accident that day? We'll never know.

Courtship, wedding, and honeymoon, all within two years. The timing couldn't have been more perfect.

His practice had steady patients, and not only that but Frankie been promoted to head chef, and she became pregnant as well.

D'Artagnan did not come into the world crying. Oh, he was an alert baby, but crying, he did not do. He just seemed to look around at his surroundings as if to take a mental picture that later would be used as one of his drawings.

Thus his life began.

From the moment his fingers held a pencil, Dar started drawing. He would draw what he saw in his room to what he saw in the streets and even draw what he saw in his mind.

His father knew how creative Dar was and he thought it was just a hobby of his and once it was time for him to graduate from high school, he would go on to college to become a doctor like the other men in his family. His mother, on the other hand, knew that Dar had inherited his creative side from her and decided to speak to Joshua in private about their son.

"Why not let him take two years off from school to find that special niche he has always been looking for without any pressure from us to go to medical school?" Frankie said.

Joshua's eyes widened with concern. His dream about opening a practice with his son was slowly fading before his eyes.

"Let me finish," said Frankie. "Once the two years are over, and if our son hasn't made any progress with his career as an artist, he'll go to medical school to become a doctor, and his drawings will become a hobby."

Once Joshua agreed to this plan, they had a family meeting, and Dar was excited to begin the next chapter of his life.

Dar enrolled in art school to get his creative juices flowing. Nothing! A whole day sitting behind an easel with nothing to show for it.

His teacher saw how disappointed he was and told him that it's normal to have a "creative block" for a few days and to not let it discourage him.

Dar didn't want to tell his teacher that he was on a strict time schedule and didn't have time to waste, so he just listened and nodded at the appropriate times. Dar thanked the teacher for her time and left.

Lucifer had been lurking around the world, looking for victims and had his eyes on Dar for some time.

He knew how low Dar was feeling and needed that boost of encouragement, so he felt this was a perfect opportunity to get into Dar's head.

As Dar was walking home, Lucifer strolled up to him and started a conversation with him. "What if I told you that I could make you the greatest artist that had ever lived?" Lucifer asked.

Dar thought he was just another teacher at the art school who had heard about him blanking out, and so he had asked him how. Lucifer preceded to ask him if he had ever visited the garden of Eden.

Dar felt silly to say no. Not only was the garden of Eden in the same country that he lived in, he had heard about the magnificent colors that not only surrounded the garden but also of the numerous types of trees and fruits that were in the area. What a dream background this could be for any artist, no matter what your choice of media was used!

Now Dar knew from the talks that kept going from generation to generation about the tree of knowledge and how his grandmother Eve had been tempted by a "snake" to try to eat the fruit but was stopped by Adam and how others after that tried to enter as well but were stopped by the angels.

Dar had no idea that this well-dressed man who spoke like one of his teachers was the same "snake" that tried to deceive his grandmother.

Lucifer explained to Dar the same thing that he had told Eve. He told him that if he ate the fruit that he will not surely die. Lucifer also said, "For God knows that in the day you will eat of it your eyes will be opened, and you will be like God, knowing good and evil. Not only would you be like God, you would be just as good as an artist as He is because you know He created the world, so He must have a great sense of creativity and to share that with you Dar, what would be so wrong with that?"

Dar thought about it, and since he was on a deadline to prove to his parents that he indeed had what it takes to become a great artist, he agreed with Lucifer that he would attempt to break into the area where the tree of knowledge was kept and would take a bite of the fruit that would open his eyes to the true knowledge of how to become a great artist.

That night while Dar was sleeping, Lucifer snuck into Dar's bedroom and had begun very softly speaking ideas into Dar's head about how to enter into the area where tree of knowledge was.

The very next day, while Dar was sitting at his easel at school for what had seemed to be hours without drawing anything, all of a sudden he became excited and couldn't contain himself and started drawing without even slowing down. When he finally caught his breath and looked down at his drawing, he was perplexed.

He didn't understand why he would sketch an outline of a person standing outside gates that were locked with chains that he had never seen before. Through the gates, he saw a tree standing that had beauty that could not be described with words, only by drawing, using colors that he had never used before. As an artist, Dar enjoyed using charcoal colors—blacks, greys, and whites. When he finished admiring the work he had done, he finally looked at the sign at the top of the gate, which read, "Tree of Knowledge," "No Trespassing Beyond This Gate!"

Once Dar saw what he was capable of creating without eating the fruit, he was even more determined to create a plan to get beyond those gates and see for himself what he was missing.

That afternoon, once his classes were finished, Dar decided to go to the library to do some research. He had an idea of what he could possibly do to break into the area where the tree of knowledge was, but he wanted to make sure his idea would work.

Dar had heard about someone who had invented a type of explosives in the mid 1800s, and even though in China it had been used for many centuries prior to this, and it was mainly used for fireworks, he wanted to check it out.

During his research he discovered that out of the many uses this explosive called dynamite was carefully being used for, Dar was interested in only two. Construction and blowing out holes in mountains for laying down tracks for the newest mode of transportation called a train.

Since the spirit of deceptiveness was not around, Dar borrowed a wagon from a farmer who does business with the restaurant where his mother works and went to the construction site a few miles out of town. This construction site was known for storing small amounts of dynamite just in case it was needed. Dar had explained to the foreman that he was an artist and wanted to sculpt using raw material and needed a few sticks of dynamite to create such an exhibit of art of out rocks. It didn't hurt Dar either when he had mentioned his last name to the foreman.

After Dar bought the dynamite, he loaded the wagon and proceeded to the job at hand—to blow off the gates that protected the tree of knowledge!

Dar had a long night ahead of him, and every time he felt that he needed to rest, he remembered the last drawing he had done and that added adrenaline. Fuel for his soul.

It took about five hours by wagon to find the garden of Eden which was closed since it was after visiting hours. Dar thought to himself, *What a shame that I came all this way and not able to enjoy this sight. Maybe another time*, he thought.

A few miles down the road were the gates that enclosed the tree of knowledge. Since the drawing that he did of this place in class was remarkably close to what it looked like in person, he felt it confirmed that he was doing the right thing.

Dar proceeded to use the dynamite exactly the way the foreman at the construction site advised him. He instructed him to tape a few sticks of dynamite together creating a bundle, place it exactly where he wanted to on the gate, ensure that the fuse was long enough so when it was lit, he could safely get way and hide with plenty of time to spare before the explosives went off.

Everything went according to his plan. Once the explosives went off, and the smoke had cleared, Dar was more than ready to enter where the tree of knowledge was and eat because he really was hungry after all that traveling.

Can you imagine the excitement that Dar felt as he was entering the secluded area where the gates were just blown off? And as he went further in, his head was in the clouds just thinking about his future as the world's greatest artist, he ran into an angel!

Dar, in all his planning, completely forgot what Lucifer had said about the tree of knowledge being protected both by man and heavenly beings. All he remembered was about the first gate!

The angel looked so imposing with his sculptured looks, his height of seven feet, and handling the sword of flames that all Dar could do was back up, turn around, and run for his life.

The angel had a smirk on his face as if to say to Dar, "Really?" Since Dar wasn't the first nor probably the last person to try to enter and because they had strict orders not to harm anyone unless they posed a threat to the tree of knowledge, he let Dar go.

Once Jedi finished reading about exploits of D'Artagnan, he started compiling notes on his computer, writing down what Dar did wrong and how he would have corrected that mistake.

Jedi scanned through quite a few more entries about people who tried and failed to enter where the tree of knowledge was, but none of them really had piqued his attention until he started reading about Sienna.

Sienna, 2020

S ienna's family had migrated to a small island off of Greece called Sirenum Scopuli which was known for its people creating such heavenly music with either instruments or their voices. It was said it could put anyone or anything to sleep.

After Lucifer worked with several men who utterly failed at their attempt to enter, he thought he would try his luck again with a female. Sienna.

Lucifer knew that he was the best at what he did and decided the next time he would try his luck with someone he could relate to and what he was most comfortable with, that is, of course, music.

After all, he was kicked out of heaven because he was too prideful, believing that he was the best of the best.

According to The Book of the Law, Lucifer was an anointed angel who had a high office with authority and responsibility to protect and defend the holy mountain of God. The high order and specific placement of Lucifer prior to his fall allowed him a unique opportunity to bring glory to God. His role included leading heaven's choirs to worship the Most High. His fall was that he wanted to have all the glory for himself, hence getting kicked out of heaven!

Because Sirenum Scopuli was known worldwide for its music, Lucifer thought he would take a trip to that country.

Day after day, Lucifer would walk the halls of the world renown music observatory, the Polyhymnia Observatory, which means very musical or many hymns, looking for his next victim.

Patience is not a something Lucifer knew about, so when he heard the sound of Sienna's voice coming out of a classroom, he bolted toward the room and came to a screeching halt when he noticed the name of the room, Heavenly Hall, and below that, someone had written a note: "Where Angels Are Taught To Sing."

The note was taken down and ripped apart in disgust by Lucifer, and even though he was tempted not to enter the classroom, he did anyway.

What he heard was beyond anything he had heard before, and remember he's heard angels sing, so he sat down at the back of the class room and waited for class to end.

Once class was over, Lucifer quickly caught up with Sienna and began a conversation with her. Sienna assumed because he spoke about his love for music and the way he was dressed, that he was an instructor at the observatory. No one in the years that she has been a student had an intense look in their eyes, or spoke with that much passion about music.

This time Lucifer had a different approach. He had asked her if she ever thought about being the most famous soloist in the world, and when she replied "No," He proceeded to tell her about the tree of knowledge.

Lucifer explained to Sienna the same thing that he had told Dar. He told her that if she ate the fruit that she will not surely die. Lucifer also said, "For God knows that in the day you will eat of it your eyes will be opened, and you will be like God, knowing good and evil. Not only would you be like God, you would sing on such a higher level than any of His angels!"

That last sentence got her attention.

Lucifer is an expert at deceiving people where they are the most vulnerable.

Everyone in Greece was required to study and learn about The Book in school, and though Sienna was an exceptionally bright student, the only part of the course that she remembered was that an angel who was in charge of the heavenly choir was cast out of heaven.

After listening to Lucifer, Sienna's mind was racing a mile a minute. *What could I do with that much fame? how could I influence other singers around the world?* On and on her mind went as she kept thinking of other scenarios that would lead her to tell Lucifer yes! She would do it!

Sienna wasted no time in doing her research. She knew getting past the security made by man would not be the most difficult but by the heavenly security. The angel!

What kept her going throughout her research of the tree of knowledge was that she kept thinking to herself if she could taste the fruit, then her voice would be even better than it is now.

Lucifer had chosen Sienna not only because she excelled in music but because she was also intelligent.

She did her research in finding out how often the angels rotated and decide to approach them about thirty minutes before the shift ended and would begin singing. That part seemed easy enough, but how would she get past the man-made security?

By the year 2020, fiber optic beams had been put in place for protection for the tree of knowledge. The optic beams which could not been seen by the human eye and were controlled by computers that randomly created sequential pattern day after day to prevent a break in. The patterns were intricately created that by the time the pattern could be duplicated, it would be time for the entire security system to be upgraded.

Once Sienna discovered that the fiber optics are tiny strands of glass that transmit the light which controlled the security system, she knew she had a plan! She would use her voice to break through the fiber optics and then on to the angel.

Sienna booked herself a flight to the garden of Eden and off she went, in search of the tree of knowledge.

Since the majority of the garden of Eden was available to the public, the area where the tree of knowledge was kept a few miles down the road on the same piece of property.

Words could not describe the beauty and the scent coming from the garden of Eden. Where Sienna lived, that was beautiful, but compared to the beautiful colors and the scent of the flowers and fruits of the garden of Eden, her hometown looked like it had been white-washed without any fragrance. She had to shake herself to remind herself of the mission which was exactly the reason why she was there.

Once she came back down to earth, so to speak, she had remembered that she had calculated everything to the last second. As it was closing time, she needed to find the path that led to the secure area where the tree of knowledge was kept.

Sienna began singing. Even though the song had not yet reached the correct pitch to break the fiber optics, it had such a melodic tune that as she was singing to herself, she hadn't realized how much time had lapsed since she had first began singing, and once the correct pitch had been obtained, the fiber optics had been broken.

Startled, once she realized that the doors to the manmade security gate had opened, she entered. Once inside as she continued singing, she also hadn't realized that the sound of her singing had been carried to the angel who was sound asleep. *Mission accomplished*, she thought to herself.

This was one test that Michael did not put his angels through—the sound of beautiful music.

It was so sad that the watch that Sienna had worn was always set five minutes behind on purpose. Even though pride had not yet entered the world, Sienna enjoyed the way people greeted her when she attended functions to which she was always late for. She didn't even give it a second thought.

As she continued to sing and stare at the angel who was so beautiful and thinking she had five more minutes before the changing of the next angel would take place, before she could get to the tree, seeing how serenely he was sleeping, she took a step closer to get pass him. No sooner than she cautiously took one step past the sleeping angel, another angel comes in, flapping its wings with the sound of a crashing wave to replace the sleeping angel. The force of the angel's wings was similar to a gale wind that sent Sienna back outside the man-made security gate unharmed! Nothing hurt but her feelings.

Man, thought Jedi after he finished reading about Sienna's escapade, *I sure wouldn't want to have been that angel on duty at that time, trying to explain to his boss what happened. Poor Sienna, to get so close, yet so far.*

"Ready to go home, son?" he heard his father call from the doorway, bringing him back to the present.

Home? thought Jedi to himself. *Already? I didn't even eat lunch.* Jedi was so engrossed in his work that time slipped by so fast he forgot to eat.

Jedi couldn't wait to come back to work the next day.

Jedi

J edi tossed and turned all night long. He wasn't nervous about his
second day on the job, just the opposite. He was anxious about
devising a security system which would surround the tree of
knowledge to prevent people from ever entering again, so the world
would never need to worry about intruders and forever live in a state
of utopia.

Felix was both shocked and happy to see Jedi already downstairs, dressed and ready to head off to work with him.

"A little nervous, are we?" asked Felix with a huge grin on his
face.

"Not at all, Dad," Jedi continued, all excited. "With all the
research I did yesterday, finding different scenarios people tried to
use and get past both security systems for the tree of knowledge and
failed, I can't wait to start writing down my theory, and even better
yet, I can't wait to go to Israel to test it out in person."

At the last statement, Felix had to compose himself. Even
though he and his son talked about him creating a highly advance
security system, and Felix knew his son was capable of doing something like this, but number one, he didn't think it would happen so
fast. Number two, how did Jedi assume he would be the one to test
the system, and number three, the most difficult one to think about
was Ruth! How will they convince his mom that Jedi was the only
one who might be qualified to test out the system alone?

Well, thought Felix to himself, *we'll have to cross that bridge when
we come to it.*

Jedi was already in the car before his dad, and his mind started
racing as fast as his dad's car engine.

Before Felix could turn off the engine, Jedi had already jumped out of the car, racing down toward the building to start on his project!

"See you after work, son," Felix had to shout because Jedi had already gotten so far ahead of him. "And this time don't forget to take your breaks and eat lunch," Felix added.

Jedi quickly said hello to his co-workers, unlocked his computer, and feverishly started typing down his thoughts as though he was afraid he might lose his train of thought.

Sienna had the right idea about the fiber optics for the man-made gates, Jedi thought, *so let's start there, and as far as the angels go, boy do I have something for them.*

His second day at work was exactly the same as the previous day, with the exception that Jedi had to stop for a brief moment when he was being introduced to another co-worker who started that day.

Deja vu. His father stuck his head in at the same time and said the same thing as the day before. This time he needed to print out what he had written. As he was shutting down his computer, he realized that the darkest pair of brown eyes that he has ever seen were staring directly at him.

"You must be either the best-looking robot that I have ever seen or just someone that really enjoys his work."

Those eyes speak, Jedi thought to himself, as the eyes continue to speak. "We were introduced early this morning, but you were so engrossed in your work, the only thing you said was 'hi,' and you promptly went back to work. Let me properly introduce myself to you again. My name is Nine," she said. "And yes," she answered before Jedi could ask, "like the number."

When Jedi heard someone loudly clearing their throat, the trance that he was in was broken, so he had no other choice but to look away from Nine to see his dad standing at the door, pointing to his watch, indicating it was time to go home.

Jedi stammered, "Uh, it was nice meeting you, Nine, and I'll see you tomorrow. By the way," Jedi continued, "my name is—"

"Jedidiah," Nine said interrupting Jedi. "One of us was paying attention when we were being introduced."

Not only did Nine have nice eyes, she also has a smile that makes her eyes light up, Jedi thought to himself. "Sorry, tomorrow I'll promise to try and do better," Jedi said to Nine.

"Did I just see my future daughter-in-love?" calmly asked Felix.

"What!"

"Come on, Dad," said Jedi with the pitch of his voice sounding a little too high to be convincing. "I just met her. Anyway," Jedi said with his voice returning to its normal pitch and changing the subject, "have I got something to show you!"

Once everyone had eaten dinner, Jedi and his dad had some time to be alone. Jedi took out his papers and showed them to his father.

After Felix read Jedi's paper, he looked at Jedi with tears glistening in his eyes, and of course Jedi immediately thought the worst.

Felix put the papers down on the coffee table, looked at his middle child, who had always underestimated himself, with such a loving look and said, "Jedi, I think that you're on the right track." Those simple words that Jedi heard from his father was all the motivation he needed to get the job done.

"Tomorrow, son," Felix said "I want you to promise to take your breaks and a lunch. Since you know that you're on the right track, it's okay to take a breather and we can't have you being burnt out before you accomplish your goal and what a better opportunity for you to get to know that young lady better?"

"Nine," said Jedi.

"What, son?" asked Felix. "Did you ask me if it's nine o'clock?"

"No Dad, 'Nine' is her name," replied Jedi, "and yes, I'll start taking my breaks and going to lunch. Good night Dad," said Jedi, and Felix replied, "Good night, son, and what a great job you did today."

Felix couldn't wait to have his nightly "pillow talk" with his wife. This is the time that he and Ruth could unwind and tell each other about their day.

Ruth had already completed her ritual of washing her face and brushing her teeth and was waiting in bed for her husband to come in to do the same so they can share their "pillow talk."

As Felix was brushing his teeth, he was so excited that he was talking as he was brushing his teeth, and poor Ruth couldn't understand a word that he had said. Ruth hadn't seen that type of excitement in Felix in such a long time, that she didn't have the heart to stop him, so she just patiently waited until he finished brushing his teeth and came to bed where they could have a face to face conversation.

"So what do you think, babe?" Felix excitedly started.

"Well to be honest, Felix," started Ruth, "I couldn't understand a word you were saying because you were talking while you were brushing your teeth, and I knew that in itself was something you never have done, so I just waited until you were finished so we can talk.

"Our son," began Felix, "has possibly come up with the greatest idea to preserve our world as we now know it!"

With that, Felix proceeds to tell his wife of what their child has accomplished in just two days on the job.

****

The next morning, Ruth is up before anyone in the house and has prepared all of Jedi's favorite things for breakfast—pancakes with a hint of vanilla, both bacon and sausage, and scrambled eggs. Coffee brewing for her husband.

Even though the aroma of the delicious smells was traveling throughout the house, Jedi wasn't prepared to see the spread that was set before him on the kitchen table. During the week, it's usually cold cereal and/or toast with juice. This type of extravaganza was saved for the weekend or when all the kids come home to enjoy it.

"Come and sit down, son. Your dad has told me that for the past two days you have been so engrossed in your work, that you haven't been taking your breaks or even going to lunch. At least this way," his mom continued, "I know that you've started your day right with a good breakfast."

"Thanks, Mom," said Jedi, and as he sat down, he saw the same look in his mom's eyes that he did yesterday in his dad's. Admiration.

Once breakfast was finished, Felix and Jedi said their goodbyes to Ruth with hugs and kisses and were on their way to work.

During the ride to work, Felix told Jedi again how proud he was of him and for him to take his time with the project. His dad emphasized that under no circumstance should he share his project with anyone, with the exception of he and his mom. Jedi promised.

Over the course of the next few months, Jedi worked constantly on creating *The Plan*, and true to his word, he did take his breaks and his lunches.

It was during these times that he learned more about Nine and became more intrigued with her and decided it was time to ask her out on a real date instead of just talking at work.

Jedi was impressed once he found out where Nine lived. Not only did she have a nice apartment but she lived there alone.

He remembered her saying that Italian food was her favorite type of food, so he went on the internet to see who had the best Italian food in the area, and he definitely was not disappointed.

The ambiance! As soon as you walked in, you had the sense that you were in Italy. In order to get to the hostess area, you had to walk over a bridge and under the bridge. Not only was there water but gondolas, and if you listened closely, you could hear the gondolier softy singing and strumming his guitar.

Score ten points for Jedidiah, who has never had a serious relationship nor did he ever have the confidence that someone would actually be interested in him!

As they were looking over their menus, the waiter came up and asked them if they were interested in ordering some wine. Since this was Jedi's first time having wine (his father had given him some tips before he left), he asked the waiter what he would suggest, so Jedi went with the waiter's recommendation.

Once the waiter returned to their table with the wine, Jedi and Nine proceeded to slowly sip their wine. The wine was a hit!

As they waited for their food to arrive, Nine began the conversation asking the normal first date questions. How old was he, how many sisters and brothers did he have, how long has he been working at the lab, and what was the current project that he is working on?

All those questions were easy enough to answer with the exception of the last one. Jedi had to think long and hard before answering that one! He had remembered what his dad said about not telling anyone about his project, and with the combination of the wine and the fact that the lying spirit was not yet around, Jedi proudly began to tell Nine what his project was.

By the time their food had arrived, both the conversation and the wine flowed freely.

All the waiters knew the effect of drinking too much wine, so their waiter suggested they both drink coffee to take away that sensation that they weren't used to feeling. They both agreed and had several cups of coffee before Jedi paid the bill and left.

Jedi's date with Nine was a success!

Their conversation continued about his project until they came to her apartment. Once Jedi had walked her to her door and was getting ready to tell her what a nice time he had, he wasn't prepared to hear the next words coming out of Nine's mouth.

"I would love to go with you to Israel to record and help document each and every step you take for *The Plan*," said Nine. "This way," she continued, "not only will you have documented the proof, but I'll be able to share this exciting time with you. I know this caught you off guard, but once I heard about it, I knew that I wanted to be a part of this, so please think about it, go home and talk it over with your parents, and let me know in a few days."

All the way home, Jedi mentally began to make a list of pros and cons of the reasons of taking or not taking Nine with him.

The pros were easy enough to come up with he thought. *I really admire her work, she's excellent company and easy to talk to and she actually might be "the one." What better way to see how we communicate by spending a few days together?*

The only con he could think of was, what if *The Plan* didn't work and then he would look like a complete failure in Nine's eyes? His confidence quickly resurfaced as he said to himself, "Nah, that won't happen."

Once he made it home and saw that the light was still on in the living room, which meant either one or both of his parents were still up, it made his decision easier, but first he wanted to run it by his parent to see what they thought. Little did Jedi know, the reason why his parents were still up was because they wanted to hear how his date went and was not about to wait until the next day to hear all about it.

"Mom, Dad," Jedi started.

"How did your date go?" both parents interrupted Jedi and asked the same question at the same time.

"Well, actually that's what I want to talk to you both about," said Jedi.

"Oh, this sounds serious, son," said Felix with a huge grin on his face.

"Should we sit down?" asked Ruth, to which Jedi replied, "yes."

Jedi started describing his date to his parents from the beginning of entering the restaurant, the ambiance, the drinking of wine and the meal itself. He continued telling his parents how easy it was talking to Nine, at which Felix and Ruth both lovingly looked at each other bringing back memories and how Jedi said both the conversation and wine flowed.

"What I did," said Jedi, "was tell Nine about *The Plan*." His parents weren't shocked because the same thing happened to them on their first date—not that Felix had some top-secret project that he was working on but how they talked all night. "And," he said with a long pause and quickly finished, "she wants to come with me to record and document everything,"

"Well," said Felix, "I did hear from Nine's supervisor that the work that she has been turning in is excellent, and Nine is one of her best employees. And not only that, they have been trusting her with quite a number of high-profile cases." Felix asked Ruth, "What do you think babe?"

Ruth, looking with that concerned look on her face that only a mother could have, slowly began saying, "Jedi, the fact that you thought enough to ask us our opinion on the subject shows me how much you have matured since you've been working. My only request is that you bring Nine over for us to meet and get a chance to know her better."

Over the next few weeks, Jedi began bringing Nine over to the house, and everyone felt so comfortable with each other, it was as if everyone had known each other for years.

On one special evening, Ruth and Felix thought it was time for Jedi's siblings to meet Nine. This would be the final test to see if Nine would run for the hills or stand her ground as Jedi's siblings could be a little rambunctious.

As it turned out, Nine herself was the middle child of five, but the exception was that her four siblings were all boys, and they treated Nine like she was one of them. Needless to say, Nine had a ball with Jedi's entire family and had passed the last test with flying colors.

During all this "family time," both Felix and Ruth had time to observe the dynamics of the family and had talked amongst themselves and thought that it would be a great idea for Nine to go to Israel with Jedi.

Once the rowdy crowd had left, and there was a resemblance of peace in the house, Felix and Ruth sat Nine and Jedi down on the sofa to tell them what their decision was.

Holding hands on the couch wasn't the only thing Jedi and Nine were holding, they were also holding their breath. Felix had noticed this and quickly told them to breathe. He said this quickly in order to not hold them in suspense any longer than necessary. "Your mother and I, after observing the two of you for the past few weeks, think it's a great idea for the two of you to have this adventure together so." Felix quickly went on, "So I took it upon myself to call a meeting with both of your supervisors, gave them a copy of *The Plan*, explained why it would be a great idea to send Nine along to capture the entire event on film, and once they read *The Plan*, they agreed with me!" Felix ended with saying excitedly, "So pack your bags and equipment, kids. You'll be leaving for Israel at the end of the month!"

****

The next month seemed to go by like a whirlwind for both Jedi and Nine. They both knew that this was a chance for them to make their mark in history and had to make sure they didn't forget anything that they would need for the trip.

Ruth and Felix had a "good luck" dinner for Jedi and Nine that included Nine's parents, her siblings, along with Jedi's siblings.

This was the first time everyone met, and after all the introductions were done, both families interacted as though they've known one another forever—laughing, having fun telling stories about Jedi and Nine's childhood.

Between being embarrassed by their sibling's stories about them and the feelings of being anxious, plus anticipating their future, all they could do was just sit on the couch holding hands, staring at their family members.

Everyone was having such a great time, time slipped by, and before they knew it, it was past 1:00a.m.

Saying their goodbyes to their family was going to be harder than they ever thought it would be, especially since this was the first time either one of them had ever left home.

Once all the "how proud we are of you" speeches were over, Jedi and Nine couldn't wait for the next day to start so they can begin *The Plan.*

****

We've heard that we each have our own "guardian angel," and in the past, there was no exception.

Because the population continued to grow since Adam and Eve, and because all the angels were created at the beginning of time, and they don't procreate like humans, the ratio of angels to humans was getting out of hand. Michael and Gabriel had to loan out of some of their best angels to walk with the humans. On the other hand, those angels who couldn't pass the test to become guardians for the tree of knowledge were called on occasion for back-up to guard the tree of knowledge.

These were the days when Michael and Gabriel found themselves to be the most nervous because even they had to leave periodically to watch the humans and could not be anywhere near the tree of knowledge.

It was one of those times when the back-up angels were on guard when Jedi and Nine were able to get in.

The Plan Put in Motion

Both Nine and Jedi were more than surprised when Jedi's plan didn't work, and they were able to get by both the man-made security gate and the angel that was guarding the entrance to the garden of Eden.

Jedi looked at Nine with a look that was sheer disappointment. Nine, always being optimistic, reached out to take his hand and said, "Look at it this way, Jedi: yes, your plan didn't work out as planned, but knowing you, you probably already know what went wrong."

Jedi, with his spirit already beginning to rise, answered with a medium-sized, confident-sounding "Yes, I think I do."

"Well," Nine continued, "what you need to do is to go back to your original plan, see where you might have gone wrong, make your corrections, and we come back and try again. 'No harm no foul,' like they always say."

"Jedi!" shouted Nine, "I have a great idea."

Jedi was almost afraid to ask, but because he had brought her all this way to take part of *The Plan*, Nine had done her part, and it wasn't her fault *The Plan* didn't work, so Jedi asked her what her great idea was.

Once Nine finished telling Jedi her idea, he couldn't stop being excited and overwhelmed at the same time.

Nine's idea was since they were already inside the area that was closed to the public, what would it hurt if they actually stayed inside, and she started filming what the area looked like? They would use the film once Jedi had corrected the glitch that allowed them to get in, and once *The Plan* had been perfected, they would use the documentary to show the world what the garden looks like, therefore satisfying everyone's curiosity, and if it does pique someone's interest even more, well, they wouldn't be able to get passed Jedi's security. It was a win-win situation all around.

Both Jedi and Nine knew of the history of the garden of Eden, beginning with Adam and Eve and how Satan attempted to trick Eve to eat the fruit from the tree of knowledge, and they knew that the two of them working together as a team that they would be strong enough to resist temptation, so he agreed to enter with Nine.

Nine proceeded to get her equipment ready and looked directly in Jedi's eyes and asked him if he was sure about this. When Jedi's answer was a confident "yes," they started walking toward the area that the public hasn't seen.

What they saw was so magnificent, they couldn't have described it if they tried. Even the description that Sienna had given of the area that she saw a few decades ago paled in comparison to seeing it in person, and they were so grateful they had a camera to capture the beauty of what they saw.

When they first entered the area, the grass was the color of a green that they had never seen before. Back home, they had "lush" grass, but here, to the touch, this grass felt like cotton, not itchy like they were used to, but thick cotton that you could actually go to sleep on.

Venturing a few miles deeper in the garden and at a distance, they saw the tree of knowledge in the middle of the garden surrounded by different types of roses and plants that they have never seen before. Just like the color of the grass, these roses were not only of colors that the human eyes had never witnessed before but the scent! The scent that surrounded the plants and roses if you were to close your eyes made you think you were in a store that sold exotic perfumes.

The only animals that were inside this area were butterflies. The butterflies at home couldn't hold a candle to the butterflies that Jedi and Nine saw. They both felt that the butterflies were curious about them as they began to circle around them. Not only were these butterflies vibrant in colors, but they were twice the size as the butterflies back home. These butterflies were slightly larger than hummingbirds and seemed to lead Nine and Jedi directly to the tree of knowledge.

To say the tree of knowledge was an impressive tree was saying the least because you couldn't begin to describe the magnitude for the tree of knowledge.

It wasn't just the size or the height of the tree or even the vibrant colors of the fruit or even the limbs, which seemed to say "Welcome" in a regal way. There seemed to be a spiritual aura that surrounded the tree.

Jedi knew from his reading that this place was special to God in that He, Adam, and Eve actually communicated quite a bit here, and once God decided to send them off to other parts of the country, the spirit of God was felt all over the world and was constantly talked about through His prophets.

As they were walking around the "tree," looking at it from all different angles and in an almost dazed-like trance, they both looked at each other at the same time because they both felt a "presence" of something or someone that wasn't there when then first arrived.

That person was Lucifer!

Lucifer had become exhausted roaming the entire world, searching for that special person to do his deceitful work, and he thought to himself, *Too bad that the angels that were kicked out of heaven with me weren't allowed to leave the garden of Eden. Then I would have help like Michael and Gabriel do.* So he felt that he would have better luck if he waited inside where the tree of knowledge was located, mainly because everyone that he convinced to enter somehow managed to fail to get pass either the man made security or the heavenly security or both, and this way he would be able to hang out with his evil minions.

Well, he also thought if he hung around in the garden of Eden, remaining close by, and someone was intelligent enough to disarm the security system and any remote chance could get pass the angel, then Lucifer would be right there egging them on. *To eat the fruit, and what a better way to kill two birds with one stone—literally*, Lucifer slyly thought to himself.

"Well, who do we have here?" asked Lucifer in his most believable, compassionate voice.

Once Jedi and Nine had recovered from the shock of seeing someone else in the "garden," they immediately asked together, "Who are you, and what is your name?"

Lucifer answered, "I am what you might call a guardian for this place."

"What happened to the snake who supposedly lives here?" Jedi asked.

At this name, calling Lucifer a "snake" made his hair bristle and his spine tense up, but he knew that he needed to stay composed and not show how he truly felt being called a snake if his plan was to succeed.

"Well, as you can see," Lucifer said, using his arm to make a circular motion, "look around. There is no one else around besides the three of us, and to answer your second question, my name is Lucifer, but you may call me Lou."

Neither Jedi nor Nine had ever read in "'The Book of the Law" that Satan had been given a name or even knew that he looked like a normal man, but they were none the less suspicious of this person standing directly in front of them and to cautiously begin to answer his questions.

Jedi went on to tell Lou his and Nine's name and how they were chosen to test out his plan to create the best defense security system for both the man-made security system as well as the heavenly security system. Jedi went on to explain that there was a glitch in his plan, and he was able to not only bypass the man-made security system but also pass by the angel in charge of guarding the tree of knowledge. What he hadn't realized was that this angel was one of the ones who had not passed the original tests given by Michael and Gabriel and was a substitute because all the other angels were busy being guardian angels over the humans.

Nine thought it would be better if she told the remaining part of the story because she saw how tired Jedi was beginning to look. With the energy that they both had when they started out beginning to diminish and jet lag starting to kick in, it was all Jedi could do to stand straight up and keep talking.

Nine finished this story by telling Lou how it was her idea since they were already inside the area of the garden. She thought what could it hurt if they actually went inside, and she started filming what the garden of Eden looked like for the world to see.

Of course, they wouldn't use the film until Jedi had corrected the glitch that allowed them to get in and *The Plan* had been perfected to show the world what this area of the garden looks like, therefore satisfying everyone's curiosity, and if it does pique someone's interest even more, well, they wouldn't be able to get passed Jedi's security system. She reiterated to Lou that it was a win-win situation all around.

Lucifer's eyes lit up once he heard the story and thought he would take advantage of the situation since Jedi was still sleeping.

Lucifer asked Nine with such concern in his voice if she would like to film the tree of knowledge from the best vantage point in the garden. She said yes without hesitation but then thought about Jedi.

Lucifer had pointed out that Jedi had laid down and was sound asleep and assured Nine that they would be back before he woke up.

Nine thought to herself, *If I had the best vantage point to film this magnificent place and be finished before Jedi wakes up, won't he be proud of the finished results, then he could concentrate solely on his project?*

"Okay," Nine said cheerfully, "let's go!"

Lucifer could hardly believe his good luck. "By the way, Nine," Lucifer said as they started walking, "as charming as the name Nine is, is it short for something else?" he asked.

"As a matter of fact, it is." Nine answered. "My full name is Ninieve. My dad wanted to nickname me Eve, but my mom knew that I was going to be an unusual child, destined to do unusual things, so Nine it was."

Lucifer thought to himself, *'Eve,' how appropriate that I might get a second chance.*

As the two of them starting walking around the garden, Lucifer had taken a piece fruit off the tree of knowledge and kept it hidden from Nine until it was the right moment.

Nine again was awestruck by the colors and the scent that surrounded her that she didn't realize that Lucifer had not taken her around in a circle as he promised but had ended up far from where Jedi had been resting.

"Well, Ninieve," Lucifer said to Nine, "you don't mind me calling you that, do you? Such a beautiful name for such a beautiful young lady." Lucifer continued, "Let's take a moment to rest here before we continue on our walk." Nine only agreed because she was also beginning to feel the effects of jet lag.

As they were sitting down on the luscious green grass, Lucifer thought this was his one and only chance to have her take a bite of the fruit. As he turned to pull the fruit out of his pocket and turned back to entice Nine, he saw that she had fallen fast asleep, overtaken by both the jet lag and the comfortableness of the grass.

Lucifer waved the fruit under Nine's nose a few times before the scent had actually woke Nine up!

For a brief moment, Nine had forgotten exactly where she was, and as she was gathering her thoughts, her stomach betrayed her and started rumbling, and she couldn't remember the last time she had eaten.

As her eyes focused on the fruit, and her stomach continued to rumble, Lucifer ask her if she was hungry as he waved the fruit under her nose.

Against Nine's better judgement, the combination of jet lag and the aroma of the fruit that surpassed the smell of any fruit she had ever smelled before got the best of her. She hadn't even thought about asking Lucifer where he got the fruit from as she took it from his hand.

Was it Nine's imagination that Lucifer's features were beginning to change ever so slightly as she was taking the fruit from his hand, or was sheer exhaustion making her hallucinate?

The fruit seemed too perfect to eat as Nine took a bite of the fruit, and the sensation of biting the fruit wasn't an experience like the fruits she had bitten into at home.

At the exact moment that she had bit into the fruit, Jedi woke up as though ice-cold water had been poured on him, even though he was dry as the Sarah Desert. He bolted straight up. The sense of something horribly being out of place was hovering all around him. He then quickly remembered where he was and wondered where Nine had wandered off to.

Just as suddenly, Jedi remembered the dream he had. He had a dream about what he had read on the computer about Adam and Eve, and it dawned on him who this person really was who just so happen to be in the garden at the same time they were.

"I have to find Nine!" exclaimed Jedi out loud, as if he wasn't alone, "before it's too late!"

Little did he know that the change in history had already started its decline.

He saw Nine in the distance standing next to Lucifer with the fruit in her hand. He started praying as he ran like he had never prayed before in his life that Nine hadn't taken a bite out of the fruit.

Once he caught up with them, he first noticed that Lucifer's whole demeanor had changed. In place of that kind, trusting face, his face twisted into something that Jedi had never seen or experienced before.

Although Jedi had never experienced "evil" before, he knew that this emotion that he was experiencing was fear.

He carefully looked over at Nine, who also had an expression on her face that he had never seen. He would come to know it as being embarrassed or having regrets, but whatever it was, he had to know if she ate the fruit or not.

"Nine," he said her name with such gentleness that she couldn't even look Jedi in his eyes. "Please tell me that with all the research that we did on this place, that you did not eat the fruit from the tree of knowledge?"

"Well," she started off, saying, "in my defense, I was so tired that I took a nap, and while I was sleeping, he"—she pointed to Lucifer—"waved the fruit under my nose, and with the combination of having jet lag and being so hungry, the sensational fragrance of the fruit overpowered me and woke me up, so I ate it."

Jedi had all these emotions that he had never experienced as he was looking at Nine. He knew by her eating the fruit, the world that they knew before they came here had just ended!

What he didn't know was that sin had entered the world! Satan's minions have been released! Jealously, envy, strife, murder, lust, lying, pride—and these are just a few of the evils spirits to name, but the major characters were sickness and death. The dilemma that he was currently facing was should he share the blame with Nine and also take a bite of the fruit or let her take the blame by herself and try to tell everyone that he didn't have any control over what she did.

He decided, with the strong emotion of protecting Nine, that whatever happened when they returned home, that they would face it together. Before Nine could stop Jedi, he snatched the fruit out of her hand and took a bigger bite than she did.

They looked at each other with feelings that they had never felt before. It was like an uncontrollable desire to be close to each other without being married. Again, that sense of embarrassment came over both of them.

At that moment they heard the sound of the Lord God walking in the garden, and they ran to hide. The Lord God called to both Jedi and Nine and asked them where they were. Jedi, still being in that protective mode over Nine and still feeling ashamed over those feelings he had for Nine, stepped out to talk with the Lord God.

God already knew what had happened. He only asked to see what the response would be.

Emmanuel
(Sin Enters the World)

Jesus woke up with His heart palpating as it has never done before. He knew the shift in history had just occurred, and the world as everyone knew it would be forever changed.

He got out of the bed with both dread and anticipation and fell on His knees as He began to pray fervently to His Father in heaven.

"Abba, My time has now come to do what I was born to do," He began. "Please give Me the strength to endure this trial and the words to which I will say."

Ever since He could remember, Jesus knew that He was different from everyone else.

Manny, Age Thirteen
(BEFORE SIN ENTERS THE WORLD)

The day started off as any usual Sunday. The family went to church, but this particular Sunday the pastor talked about a different type of subject. Salvation. This subject piqued Manny's interest for some reason that he couldn't explain, so on the way home, he started asking questions to his parents about the pastor's teaching. Little did Manny know that while he was in the backseat asking questions about the pastor's teachings, his parents were exchanging looks back and forth to each other, as to say, "I guess now is the time."

Once Manny took a breath in between his excitement, his father explained to him that once they were settled in at home, that he and his mother will have a talk. Little did Manny know that "the talk" would change him forever.

As Manny's younger brothers and sisters went their separate ways, Manny went into the family room to be with his mom and dad.

Marisol started the conversation first by asking Manny if there were any questions he might have regarding the teachings today from the pastor.

Boy do I, Manny thought to himself.

"Why would Pastor Don talk to us about salvation when no one on earth has ever done anything to be saved from?" Manny asked.

"Well," his mom started, "there have been scriptures in The Book that talked about a time when bad things would start to happen in the world, and there would be a 'savior' to save us all from that."

"That's great, Mom, but what does that have to do with me?" Manny asked.

"I think it would be much better and easier to show you scriptures from the book as we continue to have this conversation, son." Marisol went to pulled out "'The Book of the Law."

"Son," Marisol first asked Manny, "do you know how this book was written?"

"Sure, Mom, we learned at church about the prophets who heard from God and how they wrote down exactly what God told them to. Mom, they weren't allowed to add or subtract to His sayings. I remember Pastor Don telling us one Sunday that all scriptures in The Book of the Law is God-breathed, meaning that every word in the book is breathed out by God serving as an extension of God Himself.

"I see that you listen to what Pastor Don teaches," his mom said, impressed. "It's not only the prophets who hear from God." Marisol paused. "I had an experience when I was younger, and an angel who was sent from God came to talk to me."

Manny's eyes got big as saucers, but before he could ask more questions, His mom said, "Before I say any more, I would like for us to read a few scriptures from the book. Let's start with the book written by the prophet Isaiah. It says here, 'Therefore the LORD Himself will give you a sign: Behold, the virgin shall conceive and bear a Son, and shall call His name Emmanuel.'"

When Manny heard this, he began to stutter, not only because his given name was Emmanuel, but he knew that not being intimate with anyone until you were married was the norm, so he was confused until his mother repeated the part that said, "Behold the virgin will conceive." She emphasized the words "virgin will conceive." She explained to Manny, that yes, while Jay was his earthly father, God planted a seed in her while she was still a virgin, making Manny the Son of God!

It was a good thing Manny was already sitting down because he felt like he was going to faint. Needless to say, Manny, as curious as he was, wanted further proof of how his mother was trying to explain his lineage.

So she read another scripture that she had underlined prior to this, trying to prepare herself for this time.

This scripture came from the prophet Jeremiah. "'Behold, the days are coming," says the LORD, "that I will raise to David a Branch of righteousness; a King shall reign and prosper, and execute judgement and righteousness in the earth.'

"I know this is hard to understand," his mother said, "so let me put it another way. Someone from the direct line of David will rule, be known as a king, and will judge those on earth.

"Now Manny," his mother continued, "we know that everyone on the earth is related to Adam and Eve, but your father's direct line of lineage is from your great-grandfather David's side, whom you have never met."

That night when Manny went to sleep, he had an encounter with God His Father who explained his purpose of being born and answered all the questions that his mother couldn't.

Being only thirteen at this time, Manny knew he had a great responsibility to uphold, and he also knew that he had direct access to his heavenly Father at any time. But what if Manny said "no"?

He knew by spending time with God, God gave everyone free will to choose, and He would not make anyone do anything they didn't want to.

Manny decided at age thirteen he would not be the sacrificial lamb, and God will just need to get somebody else to do this. *If God knows everything, He already knew that I was going to say no, so I'm sure there's another Emmanuel out there, whose mother was a virgin and God put His seed in her too.*

When Manny woke up the next morning, he felt as if he had gone on a journey of a lifetime in only a matter of a few hours. His mother noticed the change in Manny right away. There was a sense of maturity that surrounded him that wasn't there before he had gone to bed.

Even though he had made his decision not to be "the sacrificial lamb" that he and his mother both talked and read about, he and his mother spent the next couple of hours talking about the scriptures in "The Book of the Law" and how it pertained to him or that other person.

Manny knew the purpose of that person's life, once sin entered the world, how it separated God from man, and his purpose was to pay the ultimate price, for someone who had no sin to die, be sacrificed for everyone's sin before, now, and after.

Manny also remembered another phrase his mother used for this person. It was "ransom." The Son of God would give His life as a *ransom* for many.

One of the meanings for ransom was to pay the price in exchange for something. In this situation the person would be the ransom, paying the price for everyone's sin—sin which separates man from God.

The ultimate price to pay would not only be for that person to die but be resurrected three days later to show the power of God.

God's message to receive salvation was to be simple, meaning to be saved, to have a personal relationship with Emmanuel, and in their heart, *to confess their sins and repent and say that He is the Son of God.* Having been saved will bring a restored relationship to God, which will bring a full potential for His kingdom ruling within us as we walk with Him.

This special type of relationship is what people had with God before sin entered the world and now behaving as if God doesn't exist.

The wonderful part of Manny's ministry, if he was to accept the "assignment," was that he wouldn't be left all alone and wondering what he would say because he knew that he would only say what God his Father would tell him to say.

Now comes the hard part: Manny needed to tell his parents that he will not be the savior of the world and to spread God's message of salvation.

He knew that by reading scriptures and listening to another pastor's teaching, Pastor Jerry's, that God was a loving God and wanted people to accept Him on their own and didn't want any robotic behavior from those who would come to love Him and also that everyone had free will.

Free will! That's the reasoning that Manny will use when he speaks to his parents, and he was sure that his parents would understand.

Since God knows everything, Manny thought to himself, *He already had a plan B in place since He knew that I wasn't going to accept the assignment that He had for me.*

Jedi

Once Jedi had had his encounter with God after he and Nine had eaten the fruit from the tree of knowledge, they immediately knew they needed to go home.

Even during the trip home on the airplane, they both noticed how people were behaving. Quite a few people were fidgety, as if something wasn't right with them, and they didn't know how to respond.

Now we need to remember that for thousands of years, sin was not in the world, so humans had the fruit of the Spirit instilled in them. Love, joy, peace, patience, kindness, goodness, faithfulness, gentleness, and self-control were all everyone in the world knew. Sin might have entered the world, but humans are creatures of habit, so with thousands of years of experiencing the fruits of the Spirit with one another, sinful behavior didn't take root right away.

Once the airplane had landed, they gathered their belongings and said their goodbyes before departing off on the plane, promising one another that they would call once they had time to wrap their brains around what they had done and had time to discuss with their families of what had taken place.

Jedi knew without a doubt that both of his parents would be at the airport to meet him to take him home, and he was silently praying that his siblings wouldn't be there too.

Before he could get his thoughts in line with what he would tell his parents, he heard his mother's cheerful voice. "Welcome home, Jedi!" said Ruth with so much happiness in her voice, you would have thought that she hadn't seen Jedi in over a year, when in reality it had been barely a week since she last saw her son.

Both Felix and Ruth gave Jedi the biggest bear hug at the same time, and all the emotions that he had been trying to keep under control during the flight home came flooding out like a dam that had burst.

"Whoa, son," Felix said gently, "this wasn't quite the reaction your mother and I had expected."

During his outburst and Ruth trying to console him, she had a quick second to have that "mom instinct" kick in and to know that something wasn't right and the middle of the airport wasn't the place to discuss it.

"Not now, Felix," Ruth told her husband, who knew from prior experience that his wife already had a sense that something was out of place and remained quiet. "Whatever happened to Jedi and Nine over there, I'm sure that he'll tell us all about it when we get home," said Ruth.

So as a family, in silence, linked arm in arm, mostly to give Jedi physical support, they walked out of the airport to their car.

During the ride home, the silence was even worse because at the airport, you had the noise from your fellow travelers' conversations to camouflage your feelings.

All of a sudden, Ruth came to realize that she was hearing more blaring of people honking their horns than normal, and the look on some of the drivers' faces that she saw as they drove by were unexplainable. Since she had more important things on her mind at the moment, Ruth didn't give it another thought.

"Home sweet home, Jedi," Felix said, trying his best to keep the mood light as they pulled up in the driveway, where Ruth was in the front, trying to remain calm when all she really wanted to do was crawl in the backseat with her son, hold him, and tell him that everything was going to be okay.

Little did she know that what her son was about to share with her and her husband, that nothing was so far from the truth that everything was going to be okay.

When all three had gathered in the living room, Jedi had politely asked his parents since he was physically and mentally drained if they could please talk about everything in the morning.

What could they both say but "okay"?

Jedi didn't hesitate to take that opportunity to quickly go to his room before his parents could ask any more questions.

Felix took his wife's hand and led them to their bedroom, where they knew that neither one of them would get much sleep, but what they did do as a custom each night was to hold hands as they prayed for their family, and this night was no exception.

Felix led the prayer as he usually did, beginning with, "Father God, Thank You for our son Jedi and what he has accomplished in the last few days. It seems that something heavy is weighing on his heart and we know that You already know what it is. We pray now, as his parents, that You give us the wisdom and the words to help him. Whatever may have happened Lord, we know that You weren't taken by surprised by any of this, and You will help us as a family get through this," said Felix.

Ruth promptly added, "And Father God, we ask of You now that You be in the center of our conversation and You speak through us. Even while Jedi is sleeping or trying to sleep, let Your peace that surpasses all understanding come upon him, knowing that he has You and us in his corner, and no matter what has happened, we will always love him." They both added at the same time, "Thank You God for hearing our prayers."

It was a good thing that Felix and Ruth went directly to bed without turning on the television because if they did, they wouldn't have been able to sleep.

****

The next morning started off as a normal day. Ruth was the first one out of bed and she was surprised that she had eventually fallen asleep and as she was getting dressed for the day, she wouldn't allow her mind to wander and was so ready to hear what had happened to her son.

As she made coffee, she turned on the television and was shocked to hear what was happening throughout the world.

People were dying! People were dying by the millions! No matter what channel Ruth turned to, that was the news that was being broadcasted.

From what was being gathered by those few doctors who had more experience than others, all who were dying were the ones that were "old," and their heart just stopped. By "old" were those who were born from the beginning of time; so the doctors were saying they died from "natural causes."

Ruth couldn't believe what she was seeing and hearing, so she yelled to Felix a couple of times before he actually woke up and came downstairs.

In all the years that Felix and been marriage to Ruth, he had never heard that type of urgency in her voice, so without even getting dressed, he went downstairs to see what all the commotion was about.

Her voice not only woke up her husband, it woke up Jedi.

Jedi sat straight up in his bed, hoping that the past week was just a dream, and at that precise moment, he realized it wasn't a dream, and he was about to find out that the consequences of what he and Nine had done had begun. He just didn't know to what extent.

As all three sat around the television, trying to digest what they were seeing and hearing, Jedi jumped up from his seat, turned off the television, facing his parents with tears in his eyes, and said as calmly as he could muster up his thoughts, "Mom, Dad, Nine and I are responsible for those people dying."

"What!" both of his parents asked at the same time in shock, knowing that their son would never joke about something this devastating if it wasn't true. In their wildest dreams, they couldn't imagine how this was even possible.

Felix stood up, looked Jedi in his eyes, and calmly said, "Son, does this have anything to do with your plan?" Before he could answer, Ruth who was already on her feet to have Jedi sit back down, so that they could be near one another.

"Yes, Dad, it does," answered Jedi.

"But how?" asked Felix. "We went over *The Plan* together, and it seemed perfect."

"Dad, on paper, it did seem like a perfect plan, but something went wrong." Jedi began to explain to his parents that he and Nine had followed the plan exactly, and the two of them were equally shocked when they were actually able to get in the area where the tree of knowledge was.

"Nine had a great idea," Jedi continued with his story, "since we were already inside the garden, what harm would it be for us to document the beauty of the garden and what it truly looked like from us actually being there? We thought if it was documented, it would eliminate people's curiosity from ever wanting to try to break in.

"What we didn't count on," Jedi said, "was someone else being in the garden."

The mention of someone else being inside the garden had his parents' minds racing with questions, but self-control took over, and they both held their tongues to let their son continue with his story.

"He told us his name was Lou, and you would have thought that with all the research that I had done on 'The Book' that I would have known right away that something wasn't right with this picture, but with us actually getting in the garden and jetlag starting to set it, my mind wasn't working at full capacity.

"Well, this Lou, after we told him what we were doing there, asked us if we would like for him to take us to the most advantageous spots to make sure that the video was a success that we were planning to show the world.

"Mom, Dad," explained Jedi, "words alone can't begin to describe not only the beauty of the garden but the smell and the touch of the grass! Can you imagine grass feeling like the softest pillow you have ever felt? Even that description doesn't do the sense of touch justice. For the flowers and the fruit, take your sense of smell and visual and heighten it to infinity and that still pales to comparison to actually experiencing the beauty and fragrance of everything that was around us.

"Documenting all this on film was a great idea, and if I wasn't so tired from jet lag, I would have gone with Lou and Nine. Yes, that's right, I didn't tag along with Nine and Lou to the filming of the garden because Lou said they wouldn't go that far and would be back shortly. Boy, was I stupid.

"Well, to make a long story short, while I was asleep, somehow Lou enticed Nine to eat the fruit. Her version was that between the look and smell of the fruit, along with her being hungry and tired, her best judgement went out the window just like mine did.

"I must have woken up at the same time that she took a bite from the fruit because I woke up in a sweat as if water had been poured on me, and I knew at that moment something was wrong and that I had to find Nine. I didn't know what direction to start, so I just started running, and when I saw the two of them, Nine's look of confidence that she normally has was replaced with a look that I have never seen on anybody, and the same could be said about Lou. His face had changed from having a look of concern when we first met him to another look that I can't describe, but it also was different than Nine's.

"I had two choices," Jedi said as he looked at his parents with tears in his eyes, "either to just take Nine away and take a chance that the world had not changed or take a bite of the fruit myself. This way we both would be responsible for the change of the world as we previously knew it. So I did the only thing that made sense to me. Knowing how I felt about Nine, I bit the fruit too."

"What happened to 'that person'?" his mom asked.

Jedi answered her question as best as he could with what he could comprehend in his own mind. "Once we both had bitten the fruit, he just disappeared, and as crazy as that sounds, we also had an experience with God!"

When Jedi said this last statement to his parents, they felt goosebumps on their arms.

"It was a sweet gentle breeze," continued Jedi, "that carried His voice to us and told us that since the fruit was bitten, we must leave the garden, go home, and face the consequences of what we did.

"You know," he kept talking with his parents, "you would have thought that His voice would be raised with anger or some other type of emotions, but it wasn't. It was a gentle command for us to leave. He also told us that what we have done will bring us closer to Him. How? I have no idea."

What he did know, he thought to himself, was that he needed to get back to work to see if some sense of normalcy was still there.

Mayhem throughout the World

During the next few months, so many new things were put in place.

First of all, the increase of doctors, not just doctors who were general practitioners but doctors who had specific fields, such as doctors who specialized in the heart, bones, diseases, children, and the elderly. The list went on and on. Whenever they thought a specific illness was under control, something else would happen, and they had to learn about that one.

All the doctors had to take crash courses, but mostly it was learning on the job, hit-or-miss type of situations.

Also to keep up with the high demand of people who wanted to be doctors, more schools were constructed throughout the entire world.

It wasn't just the medical field that was increasing, which also including the field about people learning about burying the dead, which was still on the rise due to people dying at an alarming rate. Something had to be done about the erratic way people were behaving. Small things at first, but still, things that were out of the norm.

For instance, telling someone something that wasn't true about something they did or taking something that they didn't pay for or that belonged to someone else.

People who were natural leaders, owners of companies, people whom others in the communities respected throughout the world met, discussed, and shared through the internet, and video conferencing meetings what type of order should be put in place to address the behavior of people. Some had ideas to divide people by cities and to choose leaders over them and certain people to decide what should happen to those who did something wrong.

What would be the consequences? Would there be a defender for the ones who were being accused?

Everyone had questions, but no one had any answers that everyone could agree on.

It was during one of these discussions that someone remembered that there was a company who specialized in not only preserving "The Book," but it was also their responsibility to keep accurate historical records as to record history as it was happening.

Archibald Baxter, Archie to his friends, volunteered to take on that responsibility and report back with more information and suggested to everyone that until that time, they write down other possible solutions.

Jedi

It had been more than a couple of months since Jedi had been back from his and Nine's disastrous trip to "the garden," and all he could still feel is disappointment and sadness in what took place.

His parents have always been supportive, but it seems this time, even they didn't have a solution but could only tell him to go to work and maybe the answer was in "The Book."

So that's exactly what he did. He kept himself busy by going through the files on his computer, that was downloaded off DVDs, and read one by one what was written about "The Book of the Law" to see what he could learn.

It was during this time that he had immersed himself in his work that Jedi was told that he had a meeting with someone who was also interested in learning more about "The Book of the Law."

Jedi met with Mr. Baxter on a Monday, and by the end of the week, he felt more alive than he had in a long time.

Mr. Baxter explained who he was and how he was meeting with other leaders throughout the world by trying to put some laws in place in order to handle the bizarre way people were behaving.

The primary reason, he explained, that he wanted to meet with Jedi was because he heard that in his company, Jedi was the expert on "The Book of the Law," and if God had put something in this book about the future, knowing sin would enter, He would have also put a plan in place that would help His people survive this catastrophe.

Once meeting with Mr. Baxter, Jedi explained that this assignment sounded doable, and he was hopeful that he could find something useful and asked Mr. Baxter if he would be able to give him until the end of the week.

To this, Mr. Baxter excitedly answered, "Yes, and I know that I won't be disappointed in what you find."

Wow! thought Jedi, after he left Mr. Baxter, *wouldn't it be great to be able to help in any way possible, be part of the solution, knowing that I was part of the reason that people are behaving the way they are?*

Jedi couldn't wait to see Nine that night after he had met with Mr. Baxter.

They continued to see one another after the "incident," but it seemed as if the spark had gone out of their relationship because they both had an emotional dark cloud looming over their heads that stopped them from enjoying each other's company as they had in the past.

Jedi and Nine

J edi and Nine both decided to meet somewhere else other than their parents' home because they didn't want them staring at them with those "pathetic" parent eyes, so they went to a coffee shop around the corner from Nine's house.

Once there, after they sat down and ordered coffee, Jedi was the first one to speak. "Look, Nine," he began, "I know that things have been a little awkward for us lately at work, and I have been trying to give you space, but the fact is that I really do miss hanging out with you, and I've been talking to God more than I ever have done before in my life. Not only concerning us but also concerning where this world is headed now that sin has entered the world."

"So has He answered you?" asked Nine, touched that Jedi would include their relationship along with his prayers concerning the world.

"Not in an audible way but inside," said Jedi as he pointed to his heart. He continued to explain before he lost his nerve or something else went wrong, as they seemed to continue to do in his life. "Today, I met with a man named Archibald Baxter and he wants me to research 'The Book of the Law' to see if God had put any plan in place for this time in history. You know, once sin had entered in the world, and people started doing things out of the norm. I told him I would, and I would get back to him by the end of the week.

"How crazy would that be, Nine," he said to her with an excitement in his voice that she hadn't heard since they talked about *The Plan*, "if we had a part helping this chaotic world be put back into some sort of normality, as much as we were also responsible for creating this chaos in the first place?"

"How can we do that?" were the only words that Nine was able to whisper.

"I believe that with the two of us researching different chapters of 'The Book of the Law,' we will be able to give Mr. Baxter exactly what he is looking for," replied Jedi.

Nine agreed with Jedi that his idea is great, but one week is not enough time for them to do a thorough job. "I know you said that Mr. Baxter had spoken to your supervisor before he spoke to you, and they both agreed he would pay for all the hours you put into this project along with any assistant that you may need, but I feel a month is a little more realistic than a week, and if we finish before the deadline, then hey, that's a plus." Nine finished saying.

"I think that's a great idea, Nine," Jedi said, to which he quickly wanted to confirm that Nine was in to assist him with his latest project. "So you're in?" he asked shyly.

"Of course," Nine answered. "How could I not want to be a part of a plan that is trying to make the world a better place, especially since I am basically the person who's responsible for it being this way?

"But also," she continued, "to be honest I really miss hanging out with you too, and I was just too ashamed to say anything to you. So this project came at the perfect time."

The hours seemed to slip by as they put their heads together to strategized how they would tackle their latest project and actually come up with a plan.

Jedi and Nine decided to each tackle "The Book of the Law" from different perspectives. Putting in key words, such as *laws*, *judges*, and *rules*, just to name a few, they came up with quite a bit of information.

They couldn't believe what they were reading. It was as if they were reading the answers to a test for actions and activities that might happen in the near future. Without trying to analyze what they were researching, they just began writing down what they read and saved it on a USB file.

Day after day as they spent time researching "The Book of the Law," they both were getting their own perspective of who God really was and how He cared so much for His people that He had already outlined His plan that would help this world put chaos back into order.

They both felt His compassion instead of rage when they had their encounter with Him in the garden, but what they were reading in "The Book of the Law" makes His compassion for the world unexplainable.

It was unfortunate that the majority of the prophets who had written chapters in the book had passed away, so they had to start their research with what was written in the book, but both Jedi and Nine also knew that God still speaks to people now.

This project took a little less than a month to complete so Jedi was grateful that he had listened to Nine and had told Mr. Baxter that he would be finished sooner than expected.

Before they handed over their file to Mr. Baxter, Jedi and Nine decided to first meet and talk about what they discovered about God.

It was strange how from the beginning of them researching, they both had heavy hearts because of what they had done, but by the end of them completing the research, it was as if God was speaking directly to them, and He had lifted some of the heaviness from each one of their hearts. At that moment, they seem to have hope to replace the feeling of hopelessness.

Trying to Put Chaos Back to Order

Archie knew that he was dealing with an expert to research "The Book of the Law" when he hired Jedi, but he couldn't believe what he was reading in just the first few pages of the report.

He had to stop reading the report to gather his thoughts, compose himself because he was so excited, before he read any further.

You see, Archie grew up in a home where God spoke to his parents. He would share His thoughts about the human race and also about the future, so they weren't surprised when chaos entered the world.

His parents in turn talked more about God and His being more than other families did with their children because they somehow knew that their son Archie would play an important part of history.

Did his parents share this bit of information with him? Of course not. Not only would this put an unnecessary burden on their son, but they could see behind his carefree personality, he was truly interested in what they were saying. Their faith in God knew that Archie would step into his destiny on God's timing and not a second before that.

Wow, God! Archie thought to himself. *You really did know that this world would be turned upside down, and because You love and care so much for mankind, You had already made a plan to turn chaos into order.*

Archie took his time reading the report and even went over it twice.

During the second reading, Archie wrote down keywords so that he wouldn't forget anything of importance as he and the leaders were to meet again.

What Archie had done was make copies for each of the leaders, had it mailed certified to their homes with a letter attached from him, saying, "Please take your time in reading the report. Jot down any ideas, thoughts, or questions that you might have, and we'll meet in two weeks. What you have in front of you, in your hands, will give you a sense of peace and a plan to help bring chaos back into order."

Meeting of the Minds

When all the leaders met, and because they knew how important this task was, it took about six months to put a plan in motion to have some type of order globally.

First it would be at the city level. The cities would be divided into districts, depending on the size of the city. Each district would have a representative in charge who would have, so to speak, the ear of the people, the problems that exists. That person would then report to the person in charge of the city, who would be called a "city manager."

The second level would be the state level. The same concept would apply here. There will be a representative from each city to meet with the head of the states to advise them of the activities and problems that also exist.

The final level would be the third level, which would be head of the country. This person would be in charge of the country and in turn would have several divisions under them to help run the country, in addition, the representatives from each state will meet on a regular basis.

The next plan on the agenda was crime or criminal offenses and activities.

The leaders also found in the report that Jedi and Nine had created that God had taken care of this area too.

What stood out to the leaders was in "The Book of the Law" were groups of people who were called judges and lawyers, and also there were laws or rules to be followed when someone stole something or as huge as someone murdering someone. Yes, murder was in the book.

In the book, they mentioned other rules or commandments from God. What primarily stood out to them was where it said, "You shall not steal, and you shall not kill," and there was to be a punishment for all crimes. If someone committed a crime, it would always be helpful if there were one or two witnesses who witnessed the crime in addition to the evidence.

We know that a person could lie about a situation to say a person was guilty merely based on the fact that they didn't like the person, so hopefully there would be more than one witness to corroborate the findings.

Based on the type of crime, it determined the punishment, and in "The Book of the Law," examples were given to help the leaders decide.

A judge would be the person who would preside over the case when a person committed a crime.

A lawyer would be the person who was familiar with the laws or rules in the book, who would either defend the person who committed the crime to say they were innocent or a lawyer on the opposing side saying they committed the crime and needed to be punished. If the person was found to be guilty, the judge would determine what the punishment should be.

The leaders came to the decision of having twelve impartial people listen to the individual cases and give their opinions based solely on the evidence that was presented by the lawyers, and it would be up to the judge to say what the punishment would be if the person was found guilty.

Who would be in charge of ensuring the public's safety and to bring those who committed crimes to the courts and where would they stay until their case went to court? The leaders also found this answer in "The Book in the Law." In the book, there was talk of war, where countries fought against one another, and the groups of people who were fighting were called armies.

Since an "army" was a group of people on a larger scale the leaders needed (at the time), they thought to bring this same type of protection on a much smaller level, again, as it was needed.

The protection levels would be designed to protect the individual cities, states, and countries. Of course as the levels grew, the protection level would grow also. You couldn't have the same number of people protecting the city as you would the states or a country.

This was just the beginning of protecting the world.

What would be the characteristics of the leaders that the people would want them to possess in order to fill these positions? They decided based on what they read in "The Book of the Law" and of the similar qualities this group of leaders possessed is what they would base their standards on—someone who had compassion for their fellowman, could be trustworthy, ethical, has high moral standards, be objective, understanding, patience, have humility and common sense, just to name a few, but one characteristic they felt was necessary that someone should possess would be a person of valor because in these trying days, it was very important that someone exhibits courage in the face of danger.

Now came the important questions. How would these people be chosen?

The leaders decided to first start with the lawyers and judges. How will they learn?

Schools! Just the same as other professions were required to go to school, why not first have an intense course for those who had showed an interest in practicing law and during this time create a curriculum for the future?

The teachers at this time would be chosen by the leaders who felt they were the most comfortable and retained the most knowledge from "The Book of the Law."

It was decided in order for an applicant to be accepted into the school of law, and because they were getting their guidelines from the book, in order to practice "law," an ethical test needed to be given first to see if they possess the qualities that they were looking for.

Once they past the ethical part of test, they would then be allowed to attend school. Otherwise it would have been a waste of time to discover that someone of high intelligence could pass the written test but couldn't past the ethics test.

After a student finished the course of studying law, a written test will be given not only about what was in the book but also what was taught at school. When a student had passed both the ethical and written portion of the tests, they would be given a certification of completion. Those who wanted to be judges needed to practice being a lawyer for a specific amount of time before becoming a judge.

Considering those in charge of protection would be held in high esteem, they also would be required to attain some type of training or courses so everyone would be on the same page. They also would be given a test to observe who was ethical or not before they could take the aptitude test.

The ethical test would be comprised of questions that would determine their sense of character and morals, and the aptitude test would be based on a series of questions on how they would handle different situations. The same scenario would apply as the lawyers either pass or fail.

Finally, how to choose those to govern over the people? One of the leaders had a great idea: vote!

Since the person would be representing the people, what better way to select them than by letting the people choose who they wanted to represent them?

Elected officials! This had a nice ring to it. The person who had the most votes would win.

Months after the leaders finished meeting, they truly felt that they accomplished something, had a sense of peace, and were ready to go to their respective regions and put these laws and ordinances in place.

Everyone knew that they were working in a gray area, and it wasn't a perfect plan, but agreed to meet every six months to determine not only how a specific situation could be improved but to find out what situations worked really well and what didn't.

Now everyone was ready to go home with a sense knowing they were part of a group that helped create some type of structure for the entire world.

Jedi and Nine

At first they couldn't explain why because all they were researching were specific words that would help Archie. Yes, by now he asked them to call him by his first name.

They remembered while they were researching, from the beginning of "The Book of the Law," it said all the words in this book were "God-breathed," which meant that all the writers had heard from God. No writers were allowed to add or subtract what they thought God might have been trying to say. (Didn't we read about this before?) Every word in this book came from God, which would explain how some of the heaviness was lifted from Jedi and Nine was because they were feeling God's presence through "The Book of the Law."

When they met a few days later, they both had a look on their faces that was there when they met each other for the first time. Joy. Hope.

Jedi was the first one to speak. "I don't know about you, but all that research gives me a reason to hope that the future isn't as bleak as I felt when we first came back from—"

"I know," interrupted Nine. "I feel the same way. Did you read that part in the book where God talked about a savior coming into the world to save mankind, to save mankind from what exactly?" Asked Nine.

"I was wondering the same thing myself," said Jedi. "And since we had a specific agenda from Archie, I didn't go any further, what about you?" he asked Nine.

"Well," Nine started off sheepishly, "since I finished my part of the research sooner than I thought I would, I dug a little deeper into this 'savior' thing that was in the book. This 'savior,' from what

I read, was the one person that God sent to earth to save us from our sins, and once we die, we could live forever in heaven with Him. But get this," she continued, "not only is He the savior, and we need to be 'reborn,' but what got me the most was that He'll also be the one to save us from going to a place called hell."

"What's hell?" Jedi asked.

"From what I read in the book, it's one of the places where your soul could go once you die, and the other place is called heaven. Once your soul goes to either place, it's there for eternity.

"Hell is a place God created for Satan and his demons to go, and He didn't design it for human souls to go there once they die. In hell, it's said your soul is constantly being tormented. It's hot beyond imagination. You can't get any rest, or water to drink. I stopped reading at that point because I was beginning to be sad again," ended Nine.

"We can't stop reading there!' exclaimed Jedi. "Don't you get it? If God created a place called hell for our souls to go once we die, heaven must be the opposite type of place from hell because if we didn't learn anything from our research, we learned that God cares enough about us to want to have a way to be with us. Remember how He could always be found before we ate the fruit, and what we read in the book, He didn't want to leave us, but once sin entered the world, it separated us from God.

"So," continued Jedi, "we need to go back to the book, Nine, to see who this savior is, since we know what His purpose is, and lastly, where can we find Him?"

Nine agreed with Jedi that they can't let this research end with souls going to hell.

****

"Nine, this is going to be harder than I thought!" said Jedi. "What we know about this 'savior' at this point is that God put His seed into a virgin, who He felt was qualified or 'highly favored' to bring this baby into the world, and it also said in the book that He will be called Emmanuel. Do you know how many Emmanuels came up in my research? Too many too count."

Jedi continued, "How do we find who was a virgin at the time of conception, and isn't that a little personal for us to ask that question? We also need to narrow it down by age, Nine, because we know that a baby that was recently born couldn't possibly be the one. Also by what region and county."

"We can't give up, Jedi," said Nine, "because it's hard. Just think what's at stake here, and you, after all, are the smartest person I know. If anyone can find the person we are looking for, you can."

Lucifer

Lucifer has been having the time of his life ever since that silly girl Nine ate the fruit. He knew that his only job was to kill, to steal, and to destroy, and he was having a ball doing it.

Since he could only be one place at a time, he had to employ his minions, lust, envy, strife, pride, lying, doubting, jealously—and these were just a few to mention—to help him accomplish this task throughout the world.

His main targets would be families. His strategy would be to find out what short comings either spouse or family member may have and use it to his advantage.

For example, we all know the key to having a great relationship is being able to communicate with one another, that is, if the relationship is to survive. This particular husband was the type to come home from work, say "hi" to his family, get his newspaper, and read until it was time to eat. In the meantime, the wife has been home all day with the kids, cleaning, cooking, and doing mommy things.

Before sin entered the world, the wife was content with the way things were and had no complaints. She felt fulfilled.

Once sin entered the world, "doubt" started entering the wife's mind. Why is your husband always so quiet? Is he hiding something? Has he met someone at work who he finds more attractive than you?

Instead of asking her husband these questions, her self-esteem starts to drop.

It was during one of those days where her self-esteem couldn't seem to get any lower, while she was out shopping, she finds someone who gives her compliments and she connects with that person on an emotional level and after some time goes by, she eventually has an affair with that person.

This affair *destroys* her family!

Satan destroys!

How about this scenario: a husband who didn't have a jealous bone in his body, that is, until sin entered the world, then he becomes the jealous type. Even though his wife has never given him a reason to be jealous, it's only in his mind, which is the way the devil and his minions work.

While at work, instead of concentrating on his job, he wonders about his wife and what she does all day long at her job.

One day he decides instead of going to work, he'll call in sick and goes to the place where his wife works, so he can spy on her.

He knows based on the conversations that they've had in the past, that she goes to lunch with a group of people in the office; however, this particular day, everyone that she normally goes to lunch with, with the exception of one male co-worker, called in sick, so it was just she and the one male co-worker. It's not looking good here!

The husband has been moody and feeling left out lately since his wife had gone back to work, and on top of that, their relationship for the past few months hasn't been what is was when they first married.

His mind begins to wonder if something was going on with his wife and someone at the job. So when he saw his wife having lunch this particular day with her male co-worker, he lost it! He immediately went back home, got a gun, came back to his wife's job, and shot the male co-worker!

Someone was *killed!*

Satan kills!

The last example. Teen-aged kids, boyfriend and girlfriend, have been dating for over one year and had never done anything past holding hands.

The guy is an athlete and hanging around his friends in the locker room where the spirit of lust enters in. They are telling dirty jokes, talking about specific girls and what they like about a girl's body and showing pornographic material. The guys would tease him about his relationship with his girlfriend because they knew they only hold hands, and they were fine with that.

This particular time in the locker room, the guys were talking a bit more than usual about "sex," and this time something began happening inside the guy's body that he couldn't explain. He knew that he and his girlfriend had a date that evening so he tried to get himself under control before the date.

They went to the movies and during the movie he leaned over to kiss her and to his surprise she didn't stop him or say no, or pull away.

On the ride home, he drove to a place that was known for kids "making out," and when she didn't ask him why they were going there, he assumed it was all right with her.

While the kissing was going on, her conscience kicked in, and she told him "no" and for him to take her home. By this time, the boyfriend was beyond the point of listening to her and all he could think of was that rage of lust that was building up in his body.

He raped her!

He *stole* her virginity!

Not only did he steal her virginity, he destroyed their relationship and killed the young lady's self-esteem.

Satan's only job is to kill, to steal, and to destroy, and he does a pretty good job.

Jedi and Nine

G od was with them every time they researched "The Book of the Law" for answers.

What they discovered was the starting point they needed.

One of the older prophets from the beginning of time was still alive! What a better way to get the information they were searching for than from one of the writers of "The Book"?

Thank goodness the computers were able to store and update births, deaths, and place of addresses. Having your address on public records at that time wasn't a security concern, and once Jedi tracked down Isaiah's phone number, who agreed to meet with them, they both asked for some vacation time, and off they went to visit with Isaiah.

They knew that Isaiah was up there in age, and not sure of the quality of his mind and health, so they decided between the two of them what the most important questions would be to ask him so they wrote them down so they wouldn't forget.

Meeting Isaiah

I saiah may have had all the modern comforts of home, television, phone, internet, microwave, etc., but you could tell he was in his element spending time alone with God. With a pencil and paper handy, ready to write down what he heard from God.

Not only was he surrounded by family who adored him, he had a grandchild named Jocelynn, who was responsible for adding to "The Book of the Law" that was on the internet, which was password-protected.

Since Isaiah couldn't see that well, and his eyes didn't adjust to the computer screen, before Jocelynn could hit "enter" on the computer, she had to read verbatim back to her grandfather what she entered. After Isaiah gave his approval, then it was entered into the computer.

Isaiah warmly greeted his two guests as they were escorted into the living room by another grandchild Taylor, who also looked after her grandfather, even if he felt he didn't need it.

Once settled in their chairs and received refreshments, Isaiah started the conversation off by thanking them for trying to find the "savior."

Tempted to ask him how he knew why they were there, they both remembered at the same time, "he hears from God."

Jedi still felt the need to explain why they were searching for "the savior," and once he finished the story, he sensed the same compassion coming from Isaiah that he sensed from God.

It was during this time that Taylor made an appearance, saying that her grandfather was on a strict resting schedule and she didn't want them to tire him out, so when Jocelynn interrupted to tell her cousin that she hasn't seen their grandfather's eyes light up like that in some time, Taylor let them know that she will be back in an hour to check on him.

It was during that hour that Jedi and Nine decided to ask their questions.

Isaiah explained what they needed to know to help them with their research, and they didn't dare interrupt him when he shared information that they already knew.

He also said the child they were looking for was born in the city of Bethlehem, and yes, while the child had two natural parents, God placed His seed into the woman who had never been intimate with a man before.

At this information, both Nine and Jedi squirmed and were thankful for Isaiah's poor eyesight.

He then continued saying that while the baby was born in Bethlehem and was given the name of Emmanuel, the person is now going by the name of Manny.

Isaiah knew from speaking with Jedi that he had access to computers which stored the lineages of each of the families since the beginning time. He explained they should research "born of the root of Jesse, born of the house of David, from the tribe of Judah."

While they both knew this sounded complicated to them and not enough information to go on, they knew someone on a personal level who was an expert in genealogy from the beginning of time—Jedi's dad, Felix!

Before either Jocelynn or Taylor could come in to remind them of their grandfather's frailty, Jedi and Nine was already hugging Isaiah goodbye so hard, they thought they would break his bones. Both had tears in their eyes when they tried to tell Isaiah what an honor it was to meet him and spend time with him, and they were grateful for the information that was given to them.

The silence back to the airport between Jedi and Nine wasn't an uncomfortable type of silence but the type of silence when you just left the presence of someone that you were in awe of.

The ringing of Jedi's cellphone broke the silence between them, and after Jedi said, "Hello," no other sound could be heard from him. All Nine saw was tears streaming down his face, so she gently took the phone from Jedi's hand and said, "Hello," hoping that it wasn't bad news from a family member.

It was Taylor, letting them know that her grandfather had passed away about ten minutes after they left. But she also said that he had the biggest smile on his face when he died as if he knew a secret no one else knew and was at peace.

With the two of them going home, again with a sense of sadness, this time was completely different. They felt a sense of accomplishment for what they had set out to do. But it was also the first time for either of them to feel the loss of someone they cared about.

This sense of lost only put an urgency in their souls to work with Felix as quickly as possible to find the "savior."

The Church
(Before Sin Enters the World)

Before sin had entered the world, there were only a hand few of pastors who spoke about the meaning of "salvation."

The two pastors that were really in tune with prophecy, end times, and "The Book of the Law" were Pastor Don and Pastor Jerry.

These particular pastors were teaching their congregations about such a time and at the same time trying to wrap their minds about what the future would look like when sin eventually did enter.

They spent all their extra time in the book to be ready once sin entered the world. They both felt that any information which they could share with other pastors or leaders of the church regarding this time in the future would be helpful, so they started a blog on the internet at the same time.

They couldn't believe what they saw once they pressed "enter"! They both had titled their blog, "Salvation, Is It Really Needed?"

Within a few hours, they began conversing back and forth on the blog and had questions for each other regarding salvation, sin, and of course the "savior."

The blog was such a success, that within six months they had over three hundred pastors who wanted more information regarding both prophecy and end times and also sharing their ideas.

Everyone seemed to have an idea that others hadn't thought of, but in the end, they were all on one accord.

How do we prepare ourselves for this?

Manny's Journey
(BEFORE SIN ENTERS THE WORLD)

During the next twenty-one years of Manny's life, and although he had already made the decision early on in his life not to be "the savior," he was still curious and wanted to learn more about "The Book of the Law" than most people his age who was connected with churches.

Ironically, he worked at the same facility where Felix worked, but because they worked in different departments, they had never met. Manny worked in the information technology department—yes, the infamous IT group that everyone holds in such high esteem.

Since he had that personal encounter with God, "The Book of the Law" took on a different meaning. It spoke directly to his soul, and for his vacations, simply because he was curious, he made several trips to visit with some of the prophets that were writers in the book to squelch that curiosity. They answered quite a few of Manny's questions regarding the future, but it seemed that the question that he most wanted to ask, never quite made it out of his mouth.

Every one of the prophets knew why Manny was there but felt that the journey he was on to find the "savior" would be in God's timing to reveal the truth.

The one prophet Manny didn't get a chance to meet was Jeremiah. Either Jeremiah's schedule was busy, or Manny had made prior arrangements that couldn't be cancelled.

Manny was adamant about not being the "chosen one," and his one consistent peace of mind was with his circle of close friends.

They all came from different backgrounds, had different occupations, but the one thing they all had in common was a love for the book, and though Manny had never shared with them about the "talk" he had with his mother, he did however share with them the talks he had with the different authors from the book, which made them even more curious about the state of the world and where it was heading.

When the group of friends got together, it was Manny who led the discussions most of the time, and it was he who seemed to know the answers to the general questions everyone had.

His friends talked amongst themselves when Manny wasn't around giving him compliments and noticing that there was something different about him, like his cousin Jonny, who they met once before. His friends didn't mind letting him take the lead, and because Manny was so humble, he didn't even realize that he was a natural leader.

Manny tried many times to put it out of his mind, but he couldn't because he knew that somewhere in the world, someone was born for one purpose and one purpose only, which was to save people from an eternal hell and to live in heaven with God for eternity.

In the beginning, when God created the heaven, earth, the animals, and mankind, He knew that man would eventually blow it and eat from the tree of knowledge which would allow sin to enter in, and yet God still rested on the seventh day. He rested because He already knew He had a plan in mind, a plan of salvation that would allow Him to continue to have a personal relationship with man, once sin to entered the world.

That plan of salvation was His Son, Emmanuel, which Manny knew was not him.

Manny had a great idea! Why don't I look for him?

The Church
(Once Sin Entered)

The week that sin had entered the world, the blogs that Pastors Jerry and Don had created blew up in a way that they didn't expect. They didn't know how to respond.

People were dying in alarming numbers all over the world, and they were behaving in ways that couldn't be explained

Everyone was searching for answers. "What do we do? Is this type of behavior in all of us? How do we answer questions about sin? What does dying mean?"

But the most important question was "Is the savior here and where can He be found?"

Before answering any more questions on their blogs, both of these men of God went away for a few days to a place where they could fast, pray in peace, and seek God for guidance and answers.

Manny's Search for a Prophet Begins
(Before Sin Enters the World)

Lately it had been hard for Manny to concentrate on his own work, knowing that all the information that he needed to locate the true "savior" was stored on the computers at his job. At his fingertips, so to speak.

At this time, he still hadn't shared with his parents about his decision, and in order to back up his claim, he needed to find the right "Manny," and he knew in his soul that time was running out before sin entered the world.

Manny knew that being in IT technically only allowed him to be part of the operational team that was responsible for the support and operations of the software system that was being used. If it didn't involve the description of his position which could be stretched to include "the technology used for the study, understanding, planning, design, construction, testing, distribution, in addition to support and operation of software, computers, and computer-related systems that exist for the purpose of data, information, and knowledge processing," Manny, who had high level security clearance; couldn't do it.

Manny had to find someone in the company who had the knowledge that he was looking for, and until that time, another option he had in the back of his mind was to talk to a prophet in person. Not just any prophet but one who had his ears to God's voice when God had told him about the birth of the "coming savior."

The prophet Isaiah was out of the question because he had just undergone surgery, and his granddaughters were adamant about him not being up to receiving visitors just yet.

What about the prophet Jeremiah? Manny thought to himself. *Every time I went to visit him, he was too busy to see me.* Manny knew from the research that he did on his own computer on Jeremiah that he was another prophet who talked about the savior in the book.

This time Manny decided to call Jeremiah before making the trip, and when he called Jeremiah's home, explained in detail who he was and why he wanted to speak to Jeremiah, he was told yes, that it was alright for Manny to visit Jeremiah.

Once being approved for vacation time, Manny bought his ticket, and off he went to visit with the prophet Jeremiah.

Meeting Jeremiah

It was surreal going to Jeremiah's hometown this particular time, knowing that he would finally get answers he needed to start his search for the real savior, not only brought him a sense of peace that he couldn't explain but also comfort, knowing that he would be helping the world once sin enters the world because "the savior" will already be prepared to do what He was born for.

Jeremiah did his own work on the computer. He may have been old, but he was one who always stayed up with the times. In fact, he felt more productive when he depended less on those who were around him, and he knew that God didn't care what method he used when writing down what he heard from Him.

Handwritten or directly being put into the database of the computer for "The Book of the Law," which he has been using for decades, using the same password that has been password-protective all these years which was also being used by other prophets.

When Manny was hugged by Jeremiah, he felt a warmth that began to spread throughout his body and wondered if it was God's presence that he felt.

Once they settled down after having a light lunch and lighter conversation about how things were with the both of them, Jeremiah looked intently into Manny's eyes and asked him, "So what brings you to this part of the world?"

This was a such a direct question and one that Manny hadn't anticipated being the first one. It threw him off guard!

During the plane ride, Manny had rehearsed many times in his head how he envisioned the conversation would flow with Jeremiah, so when Jeremiah hit him with that direct question, he had to quickly regroup his thoughts.

Seeing how uncomfortable Manny was when he asked that particular question, Jeremiah had to chuckle and said, "Not the way you thought this conversation would go?" Before Manny could answer, Jeremiah continued saying, "In this line of work, I have learned if I make my plans first before asking God, He laughs, so this way I have learned to ask Him first about the direction that I should take. Sometimes He'll share His plans with me even before I ask Him. So let's start again, shall we?" This time Jeremiah had softened his voice.

Manny felt the same compassion that was being generated from Jeremiah when they had hugged before, and he was no longer nervous to share his story.

He began from the beginning of how his mom told him who he allegedly was, and Manny took this opportunity to emphasize the word "allegedly" details of their family tree, how he was conceived, and what his purpose on life would be.

He went on to tell Jeremiah that while this was a story he truly believed, he also believed there was someone else in the world that was chosen for this assignment, and it wasn't by any means him.

"And why don't you think that you're the 'chosen one,' Manny?" asked Jeremiah, already knowing how Manny would respond.

"Well, to begin with," said Manny, "I don't think I'm qualified and another important concept is from what I do know about God is that He already knew that since He has given us free will, and I choose not to be the 'chosen one,' He would already have a Plan B in place, and with that being said, I came here hoping you can help me find the true savior."

It seemed to be hours instead of minutes before Jeremiah said anything. He knew what Manny was saying was true and that God does give us free will, but he had to be very careful and choose his words wisely of what he told Manny.

"Do you know what the rabbis in this part of the country call me?" asked Jeremiah.

Manny replied, "No."

Jeremiah said, "I'm called either 'the prophet of doom' or 'the weeping prophet' because I've been sharing with this country for decades what God has been showing me what will eventually happen to this world, and no one wants to hear it.

"Yes," he continued, "since the world is still a perfect place, and because people can't or won't believe that a time will ever exist when the world wouldn't be perfect, I didn't talk that much about it, however, I only shared with them what God wanted them to know and to put that thought in the back of their minds until the time that sin does enter the world.

"I not only shared about the ugly things that would happen," Jeremiah further explained, but I also shared the good news about hope, and that God had also prepared a way for us to live with Him throughout eternity in heaven."

"So you do know who this savior is!" Manny said as he could hardly contain his excitement.

Jeremiah took a long pause before answering Manny's question. He knew the importance of what he may or may not say to Manny would affect this young man's sense of direction. He also knew after speaking with Manny that he works with someone who not only have access to the computers which stored the lineages of each of the families since the beginning time but was an expert in that particular field.

"Son," began Jeremiah, "sometimes God will share things with me in black or white, and there's no need to pray about what He might be trying to tell me because it's laid out like a map with a light shining on it. I like those times," Jeremiah said with a chuckle. "Did you know, Manny, that God likes to tell us stories?" Jeremiah asked.

"He does?" was Manny's reply.

"Yes, He does, but in 'The Book' they are called 'parables.' A "parable" is an illustrative story by which *a familiar idea is cast beside an unfamiliar idea* in such a way that the comparison helps people to better understand and grasp the unfamiliar idea. A simple story is told, certain features of which are *parallel* to the points or principles one wishes to drive home. For example, a blind man tried to guide another blind man, and they both fell into the ditch. This illustrates that while a man leaves his own shortcomings uncorrected, he cannot help others to correct theirs," stated Jeremiah.

"Why are you telling me this?" asked Manny.

"Well," Jeremiah started, "I was going to give you a parable to help you with your question, but instead I had a nudge from God who doesn't want me to give you anything but the facts that will lead you to what you are searching for."

Manny sounded confused so he asked, "So are you going to tell me exactly want I'm looking for or not?"

"Manny," Jeremiah continued to speak to him with concern in his voice, "I know it seems harsh right now, but once you discover the truth on your own, you will understand, and yes, Son, I will be giving you facts, not parables."

He explained to Manny that when he speaks to the expert at his job, Manny can help him out by telling him to begin his research with "born of the root of Jesse, born of the house of David, from the tribe of Judah." From there it will lead him to the "savior."

Now we're getting somewhere, Manny thought with excitement. But just as quickly as the excitement came, the excitement went away because he remembered a similar conversation to this one that he had with his mother when she first explained about who he was and his heritage.

Well, thought Manny to himself, *this is a coincidence but also exciting to know that the true savior and I are related.*

He was excited to get home and begin his research, knowing that the answer that he was looking for was at his job!

"There's one more thing, Son, that I would like for you to do for me," said Jeremiah, and before Manny could reply, Jeremiah continued talking. "You have a cousin named Jonny, and well, before you start your research, go speak to him and find out what he's been doing these past few years."

"Why Jonny?" asked Manny. "I have so many cousins, so what's special about him? Other than he knows quite a bit about The Book," and as soon as Manny made that last statement, he understood. So of course Manny agreed to speak with his cousin Jonny before he began his research, and for some strange reason, he felt a sense of urgency that surrounded him that wasn't there before.

Cousin Jonny

What Manny knew about his cousin Jonny was that he wasn't like anyone else in their family. While they all shared love for "The Book of the Law," Jonny was the one who was extreme about it.

Every spare moment that Jonny had, with the exception of when he met with his friends to discuss the book, Jonny could be found reading the book.

Even though they knew Jonny had been in contact with the prophets, what they didn't know is what was being discussed. He and the prophets spent hours and hours talking about what will happen once sin had entered the world, and the prophets were also preparing Jonny through "The Book of the Law" of what his assignment would be, and from what his dear friend Jeremiah had said, that Jonny is to try to help bring comfort and hope to the world once sin entered the world by letting people know that God hasn't forgotten them and for him to talk about the "savior" and to prepare the way for Him.

Jonny doesn't remember this, but he sensed the presence of "the savior" while he was still in his mother's womb. He jumped when he heard the voice of the woman who was then carrying "the savior" in her womb.

His mother loves to tell him that story, who carefully omits who the woman was, and he didn't dwell on it because he felt God would reveal to him "the savior" in His own time.

Jonny's ministry would be to share the gospel which means "good news" to the world.

In order to do that, Jonny needed help from other people—people who would believe as he did about the gospel. They would be called his disciples.

Even though his family knew he was ordained as a preacher, he really wasn't preaching that much because he hadn't yet heard from God, telling him that it was time to start preparing the way for "the savior" nor the time to preach the word from God about salvation, delivering His people from eternal hell with a chance to repent from their sins.

God told Jonny that he would be addressing different groups of people throughout the world with his message of repentance. One group would be the genuine seekers, those who in their heart knew that something wasn't right with their life, the world, and wanted to know more. They would come to him asking questions and earnestly seeking his advice as to how they can change their life, and he would answer each of their questions accordingly. These were the people who were sincerely looking for answers and wanted to repent and change their way of life because they were aware of the wrongs they were doing.

They would hear Jonny's message about salvation, believe him, and repent and be baptized by him. Because he would use the internet to spread his message, it would spread like wildfire. People would be looking for answers wherever he went. There would be people waiting to meet him and be baptized by him in whatever body of water that was in the area, as they confessed their sins.

Jonny's message would be simple. You know you did wrong, confess what you did, repent for what you did, and be baptized. Being baptized is an outward demonstration of a person's repentance from sin and committing their lives to God.

Another group of people would be the so-called religious group called Xians. This group would be hard to convince about the Son of God, the Savior, because they knew about God through studying "The Book of the Law," even some were teaching classes, while some of them might have been around from the beginning of time when God's presence was felt all the time.

There was also a religious group who called Jeremiah the "prophet of doom," who didn't want to hear about a time when the world wouldn't be the perfect place to live in.

Jonny was patient. He knew that the time would be coming soon to put his ministry into action, and until that time, he and his group of friends would continue to meet to learn about "The Book of the Law" and be prepared once sin entered the world.

Cousins Meet Again

Jonny had learned a long time ago that God always shows up on His own schedule, and this time wasn't any different.

A few days ago, he received a phone call from his cousin Manny, whom he hadn't heard from in some time. In fact it seemed whenever there was a family gathering of some type, Manny always seemed to be absent.

Needless to say, Jonny was curious when Manny asked if he could come over to visit him and wouldn't go into details over the phone on why all of a sudden he wanted to visit.

The night before Manny was to come over, Jonny had a dream from God, and God revealed to him the reason why Manny was coming over.

When Manny knocked on Jonny's door, his heart began to race in anticipation because he knew who was on the other side of the door and what he represented. So Jonny said a quick prayer to God, asking Him to give him peace and the correct words to say to his cousin.

They couldn't believe how much time had passed once they finished catching up on family trivia, such as where everyone was and what everyone was doing, so it was Jonny who spoke first and asked his cousin why he wanted to see him.

"Where do I begin?" Manny asked nervously.

"The beginning is always a good place to start," responded Jonny.

"Do you have about a week's worth of time? I'm just kidding," continued Manny. "I would like to know your opinion about what will happen in the future," said Manny. "I know that you spent a lot of time with the prophets, and in fact, it was Jeremiah who told me to speak to you before I start my own quest."

Jonny didn't expect this to be his first question, but he wasn't surprised since God had already shown him why Manny was visiting, he knew he had to be honest with his cousin.

"Well," started Jonny, "it seems that you have been keeping up with our relatives on what and where I've been spending my time, so yes, I am already aware that this perfect world as we now know it, figuratively speaking, will come to an end. Do I know when the event will take place to cause this to happen?" At this question, Manny held his breath until Jonny answered his own question, saying, "No one knows that answer except God."

"Okay, I can accept that, and before I go any further," said Manny, "I would like you to, if you can, answer another question for me. I also know that you've spent some time with the prophet Isaiah and all the studying the two of you did together and most importantly, that you're already aware regarding the time when sin will enter the world and how it will separate God from His people, but what I really need to know Jonny is, do you have any idea who in our family is 'the savior'?

"The reason why I'm asking," Manny said so fast was because he didn't want to give his cousin time to respond before he could continue with his story, "is because I remember a time when my mother gave me a history lesson on how she became pregnant with me, even though she never, uh, you know..." Feeling the awkwardness between them, Jonny nodded his head yes. "She told me that God put me there and that I am His Son and that I have only one purpose. That purpose is to save the sinners from going to hell, and in order to do that, I need to sacrifice my life and die for them all!

"By me doing this, it will bring people and God back into a relationship, that is, if they choose to. I know that I'm leaving quite a bit out about my story, but the main thing that you need to know at this moment is that I learned in church about God not forcing anyone to do anything they don't want to do, and I can't believe that I am about to say this again, but I choose not to be a 'sacrifice' for all of mankind, and because I know that God knew in the beginning that I wouldn't accept this 'assignment,' He already had someone else in mind, and my sole purpose right at this moment is to find that person, so I can be at peace.

"You know that I work at the company where all the records of history are kept, lineage and stuff, but before I make an appointment to speak with Mr. Jamison, who is the expert in that field, Jeremiah asked that I speak to you first, so here I am."

Jonny took a long pause before responding to his cousin's question, and during this pause, he again said a quick prayer to God asking Him to give him the words to say to Manny.

"Manny," his cousin said, "before I answer your question, I would like to hear in your own words why you don't think that you're 'the one.' There is no right or wrong answer, I just need to hear your honest answer."

"Here I go again," started Manny with a deep sigh. "It's the same answer that I told Jeremiah. Simply put, I don't think I'm qualified to take on such an important role. In fact, after speaking to you and what you've been doing in the past years, I think the lineage is correct, but it took a wrong turn somewhere and that you're the true 'savior,' Jonny! Because I know that your full name is Emmanuel Jonny and you just prefer to go by 'Jonny'! Yes!" said Manny, so excited. "That's the reason why Jeremiah wanted me to speak to you first before asking Mr. Jamison for his help.

"What a relief it is," Manny continued, "to know that I am not 'the savior' but you are." Manny finished speaking, pointing his finger to his cousin.

Jonny, has never been one lost for words, that is until now. Also he didn't have the heart to interrupt Manny, so he kindly didn't say anything until Manny finished speaking.

"Well, am I right or am I right?" Manny asked, who didn't even give Jonny the option to say if he was right or wrong. Manny just assumed by Jonny's silence, he was correct.

"Manny," Jonny said, trying to calm his cousin down. "You have said so much without taking a breath or letting me speak, so let's start with your first statement. You said that you believe that you're not 'the savior' because you're not qualified. These are your words and not God's. Let me ask you two questions," Jonny continued on, "do you believe that God knew you before you were born and do you think God makes mistakes?"

As thought-provoking as these two questions were meant to be, they seemed to calm Manny down as he thought about his answers before he spoke.

"If I said yes, I believe that God knew me before I was born," answered Manny, "and no, I don't believe that God makes mistakes, what would that prove?"

"It would open your mind to the reality of what you are about to discover on your own," answered Jonny.

"Hey Jonny, I thought that once I left your home, I would have a definite answer to my question and not more riddles," Manny said with a defeated attitude.

"Wouldn't your answer be more meaningful to you if you were able to continue your own research with the starting points Jeremiah gave you?"

"I guess it would be," Manny said, as he started to think positive again about his quest. *But would this be the end or the beginning?* he thought to himself.

Before he left his cousin's home, Jonny apologized to Manny if he felt that he had led him on without answering his questions.

Jonny wanted him to feel that the meeting was productive, so he had Manny contact Mr. Jamison before he left his home and made an appointment with him in a week. Felix's appointments are usually made months in advance, but he made an exception for Manny when he explained the short version for the reason of the meeting was to find "the savior>"

Manny promised Mr. Jamison to call him back later on in the day to give him the full reason why he needed to speak to him.

Manny Meets with Mr. Jamison

Seeing that they worked in the same building, Manny was a half-hour early for his appointment with Mr. Jamison and also because he desperately wanted to have closure.

Over the phone, Manny gave Mr. Jamison a few more details but explained to him the remaining details of the research would need to wait until they met in person.

As thorough as Felix is, and history has always intrigued him, he took it upon himself to begin the research with what little information Manny had given him. Felix couldn't remember a time as long as he has been working at the company that an employee was the one requesting historical facts. In the past, it has always been private citizens or companies who requested the information for an hourly fee.

Something inside of Felix, which couldn't be explained, gave him a sense that this research would not be related to anything that he has done in the past and was eager to meet with Manny.

Once Felix and Manny introduced themselves, Manny didn't waste any time to explain what he needed from Felix. Manny was thorough when speaking with Felix. He started from the beginning with his talk with his mother when he was younger to recently visiting both Jeremiah and his cousin Jonny and ending with his decision not to be the "savior" and to find the true savior.

He spared no details and even told Felix he felt that the "savior" was closely related to him.

After their conversation, Felix was more intrigued by this request than he thought he would ever be, and once he asked Manny additional questions that would help him with the research, he told Manny that this research shouldn't take longer than two weeks.

Manny left Felix's office with the sense of accomplishment.

Felix Begins His Research

His research took only a weekend to complete!

With the information Manny had given him, in addition to the data he had gathered prior to meeting with Manny and knowing how important this research was to this young man, Felix worked nonstop during the weekend.

What was strange was once he was nearing the completion of the assignment, Felix didn't realize how much time has passed.

Sure, his wife called a couple of times to check on him to see if he was alright and if he ate, but other than those times, he worked without any interruptions and worked tirelessly.

His discovery at the end was mind blowing to say the least.

He began his research with the tribe of Judah, followed that line to David, which at that time last names weren't important. He kept following that line to the present time where two specific families which had male cousins who were around the right age that the "savior" would be at this present time.

Felix's couldn't contain his excitement as the two names appeared on the monitor. Jonny's and Manny's!

He thought back to his conversation with Manny and remembered that Manny felt that the "savior" was closely related to him, and Manny was right.

As Felix entered the last bit of data to determine which person it was, his computer froze, and he couldn't get it to work again! He tried everything he knew to do on his end that had worked in the past, but this time nothing worked.

"You've got to be kidding me!" Felix yelled at his computer. During the past year, the company upgraded all the computers' software with the latest technology and was advised that the chances of the software to malfunction was minimal to none.

Well I guess it's minimal, thought Felix.

He had to calm himself down to think about what he was going to do next. This wasn't a company-approved project and on top of that, it was the weekend and because the company was closed, Felix couldn't even call someone who worked in IT to help.

Once he had his breathing under control, he knew who he could call. Manny!

Manny worked in IT, and because Felix was part of the management team at the company, he knew it would be all right to have Manny come in to see if he knew what the problem was.

Felix felt since Manny had already assumed that his cousin was the "savior," how exciting this would be for him to actually be the one to discover this on his own, right in front of him, on the computer, in black and white.

When Manny saw Felix's number show up on his cellphone on a Saturday, his mind automatically went into overdrive!

"You already found the answer?" Manny asked without even saying "hello" to Felix.

"Well yes and no, but that's not the reason why I called," Felix said softly, and before Manny could ask any more questions, Felix rushed on to say, "The reason why I'm calling you is the research came to a screeching halt because the computer froze as I was near the end, and I'm unable to get it to start working and I was wondering—"

"I'm on my way," interrupted Manny, who hung up without even saying "goodbye."

****

Felix did not know where Manny lived, but he was surprised when Manny showed up at his office within fifteen minutes, and as soon as he came in the office, he rushed right over to where the computer was and starting working on it, without acknowledging Felix.

The computer had an automatic back-up system so Felix wasn't concerned that his research was lost, he was more concerned with what Manny saw once he rebooted the system without him being able to explain where he was in the process of the research.

Right then and there, Felix had the worse cramps in his stomach that he had ever had in his life.

He thought to himself, *No, no, no, this can't be happening to me, first the computer, now this!*

He put his hand on Manny's shoulder and asked him to stop what he was doing at the moment, so he could go to the bathroom, and once he came back, they could resume where Manny stopped.

Even though Manny wanted to say "No," he respected the fact that Felix gave up his personal time to work on the research so he said, "Yes."

When Felix returned from the bathroom, expecting to see Manny, he was surprised that Manny was nowhere in the room, and once he determined that Manny had suddenly left, his focus immediately went to the computer where he left Manny and he saw that the computer was still on and because the last bit of data had been downloaded to reveal who the "savior" was, this information was glaring back at Felix!

He now not only had the answer that he had been looking for, but so did Manny!

Manny Discovers the Truth

Manny couldn't wait get out of Felix's office any faster than he did once he saw what was glaring back at him from the computer screen, and even more importantly, he hadn't touched the computer just as he had promised Felix.

His mind was numb and wouldn't allow him to process what he just learned.

There must be a mistake! He thought to himself. *Computers are only as good as the people who input the information, and people make mistakes.*

He was trying to deny the information that he saw. *By any means necessary*, he thought.

It was all he could do to not drive like a maniac and drive within the speeding limits. At this rate, he thought he would never make it back home, to the security and comfort of home, knowing he could hide out there.

For how long? Only God knew the answer to that.

Once home, too wound up to eat or relax, Manny decided to go over the information again that he saw at Felix's office. Thank goodness he wasn't that rattled by the incident to have the wherewithal to take a picture of the screen.

Manny started going over in his head the facts for checks and balances. Every time there is a birth, it is recorded, not only who the parents are, but it was also added to one of the twelve tribes of Jacob.

I know that I am from the tribe of Judah, and so is the savior. Check. And so is Jonny. I skimmed through all the generations until I got to our paternal grandfathers and slowed down at Mattan. I remember my mom talking about him. Grandfather Mattan had two sons and their names were Leland and Jacob. I know that Jonny's grandfather's name was Leland, and mine was Jacob, but Jonny's dad's name is Masai, and mine is Jay. Jacob had a son called Joseph. All this time I thought his name was Jay, I didn't know the initial J stood for Joseph!

The prophets prophesied in The Book of the Law of how the genealogy of the Christ, the Son of God, who would be called Emmanuel, which means "God with us" would run.

His mother would be Mary and her husband would be Joseph. Mary is just a shorter name for Marisol.

The exact wording in The Book of the Law says Jacob begot Joseph, the husband of Mary, of whom was born Jesus who will be called Christ.

"I couldn't dispute this if I tried," said Manny. "But what happens now, God?" Manny asked.

Once Manny had asked this question out loud, and He had accepted His destiny in life, there was a peace that surrounded Him that He had never experienced before.

****

Manny was exhausted by the time He went to bed, and when He woke up, not only had He fully accepted His assignment from His Father, He had a different attitude about it.

Before He had gone to bed, He began to pray and had a conversation with His Father.

During this time, God told Manny that He would like for Him to either go by His given name Emmanuel or Yeshua

Manny also knew that Emmanuel meant "God with us," or *Yeshua* with an English translation of Jesus, meant "The Lord is salvation."

He decided on Jesus, only because during His earlier years, He was known as Manny and felt the name of Jesus was more appropriate given to what His assignment will be.

That day He had a sense to go the temple and sit with the rabbis. A rabbi is a person who is a teacher or an expert on Jewish teachings, which comes from The Book of the Law. Some of them may even be prophets. So He sat with them every day for a few weeks, absorbing all that He could learn, and when one of the rabbi's mentioned the names of the prophets Isaiah and Jeremiah, He was excited to go home and talk to His Father.

That evening, He prayed and asked His Father for further direction for His life and what He heard from Him was to go see the prophets Isaiah and Jeremiah to learn more from them.

Needless to say, sleep eluded Him that night, which He would find out, would become a habit with Him.

Jesus Meets with Isaiah and Jeremiah

When both Isaiah and Jeremiah heard from Manny, who now goes by Jesus, and said that He would like to meet with them both at the same time, they couldn't wait to meet Him and called each other to pick each other's brain.

Jeremiah started the conversation with telling Isaiah that he met Jesus when He called Himself Manny, and He came to him awhile back because He chose not to be the "savior" of the world, and He was determined to find the "true savior" and believed that Jeremiah would point Him in the right direction in this quest.

"Well, did you?" asked Isaiah.

"I gave Him the information that God told me to give Him," answered Jeremiah. "No more or no less, just as we have been instructed to do all this time with our writings," he continued.

"Since the one thing that God hasn't revealed to me is when I am going to die, I never thought I would actually meet His Son before I died," said Isaiah.

"Well, the difference for me," said Jeremiah, "was even though I technically met Him already, I don't think it counts because He didn't know who He was, and we could have had a different conversation if He did."

At this point, both men just sat in silence waiting for Jesus' arrival.

When there was a knock on the door, Isaiah and Jeremiah nervously looked at one another as they both stood at the same time to go and open the door.

As Jesus entered the room, both men hugged Him at the same time, at which Jesus responded naturally by placing both His arms around the both of them.

Once they finished embracing one another, Jeremiah was the first one to speak. "I can tell by Your appearance and a sense of maturity that surrounds You now that wasn't there when we first met, that You have spent time with Your Father," said Jeremiah.

Jesus explained that yes, He had spent much time with His Father, and what was so amazing was He was so easy to talk to. Jesus also said that while He thought God would be angry with Him because He tried to deny who He was, He discovered God has a great sense of humor and He never doubted for a moment that Jesus would discover the truth about Himself and "He actually told Me He had a good laugh when He saw the expression on My face when I saw the truth staring at Me about Myself from the computer."

God also told Jesus that He was proud of the way He took on this responsibility by learning as much as He could of who He was and that when He took time to get away to serene locations, His Father met Him there.

During the next month, Jesus, Isaiah, and Jeremiah spent time talking about God and what the future would bring and also about Jesus' important role. Because Jesus had spent so much time with God before He came to visit with the prophets, it was as if the words they spoke over Him was a confirmation of everything that He had heard from His Father.

He knew what His mission would be once sin entered the world, to bring a message about hope and salvation by showing love and compassion and not judgement to anyone.

He also knew that since His time on earth would be short, it was important that He enlists the help of those He trusted that would continue to spread the gospel," throughout the entire world from generation to generation.

Jesus was grateful for the group of friends that He had remained close to all this time, and He felt that they would be open to hear about who He truly was.

It was during this time with the prophets that Jesus had invited His mother over to explain what He had been experiencing the past couple of years.

Marisol hadn't seen her Son in person for over a few months, but the look on His face was the same look He had when she had first told Him about who He was as a young boy, with the exception of a more mature demeanor.

His mother came to the realization that since her Son asked her to come over meant only one thing—that her Son would die!

The hows or whens weren't important, but what was important was even though God had tried to prepare her for this. It was understandable why Marisol broke down and cried when she said goodbye to her Son.

Jesus
(Once Sin Enters the World)

This was another morning when Jesus woke up with His heart being heavy, not only because the shift in history had already taken place with sin entering the world but also of the pain that He knew His mother must be in. By spending time with His Father, He also knew the compassion of God and eventually His mother would have a sense of peace that she couldn't explain regarding her Son's mission.

Today He was meeting with twelve of His friends whom God had shown Him would be His disciples, ones who would have the courage to spread "the gospel" now with Him and also once He died, but of course He couldn't tell them in the beginning that He would soon die.

Who would want to be in a group with an important mission to accomplish if the you knew from the beginning the leader was going to die?

Felix Meets with Archie

Considering Jedi worked under his dad, he was required to keep his father informed on all projects that he was working on by giving him copies of every report that was created. This included the project that he and Nine worked on for Mr. Baxter.

Usually Felix skimmed through his son's reports because he knew how thorough Jedi was, but this particular project caught his attention. Once he read the notes they had prepared for Mr. Baxter, Felix realized the importance of this project and how the different structures and levels in the government throughout the world were being created.

It was based on "The Book of the Law"!

Yes, Felix's knowledge on the book went that deep. He couldn't believe that his son and Nine had played such a huge part in history by trying to bring chaos into some type of order.

Felix managed to take some time out of his busy schedule to meet with Mr. Baxter. That in itself was a hard task, trying to arrange a meeting with Mr. Baxter because he was such a busy man, and his schedule didn't allow that much free time either. That was until Felix told his secretary who he was, which Felix was trying to avoid, using his son's name to gain access anywhere and to anyone.

The reason Felix wanted to meet with Mr. Baxter personally was to let him know without going into details about *"The Plan"* and how working on this project for Mr. Baxter changed his son's entire outlook on life. Not only did Jedi come to work with a better attitude, he seemed to have a hope that wasn't there before working with Mr. Baxter.

Felix was ushered into Mr. Baxter's office by his secretary, and the two men shook hands then hugged each other like they were best friends who haven't seen each other in a while.

"Well, Mr. Baxter," began Felix, to which Archie stopped him right there and said, "please call me Archie. After all that was accomplished throughout the world because of the time and effort that your son and Nine put in, it seems like we are family."

Felix didn't know what to expect when meeting with someone who had enough authority and influence throughout the world to bring together leaders from all over the world for one cause, and what he did feel when speaking with Archie was humility and integrity— qualities that some seemed to no longer possess.

"I just wanted to personally say 'thank you' from my wife and myself for giving Jedi the opportunity to work on your project," said Felix. "We see a different person now than who he was a few months ago. The young man we see now," continued Felix, "has a light in his eyes again, also has hope, and we owe all that to you, Archie."

"Felix," started Archie, "you don't owe me anything. It was a pleasure working with them both, and I can't wait to see the results of their next adventure together."

This statement brought a surprised look over Felix's face because he hadn't been given any information on a new project that Jedi might be working on. So Felix asked Archie, "Which project might that be?"

"Well, since I know this project will involve you, I'll go ahead and share with you what Jedi and Nine told me." Archie continued, "While the two of them were working on my project, they discovered that God already knew that sin would enter the world and that He already had put a plan in motion, which was called 'the plan of salvation,' which required a 'savior.'

"They decided they would go and speak to the prophet Isaiah, who wrote one of the chapters in 'The Book of the Law' to see if they could gather more information about this 'savior,' and once they spoke to Isaiah, from what he had told them, it gave them enough information to research who this 'savior' might be, but they felt overwhelmed until they realized that they already knew who would be the best person to help them with this research, which would be you!"

The look on Felix's face once Archie finished speaking could be described as shock, disbelief, and bewilderment, changing into humility. Humility, knowing that his son thinks highly enough of him to want them to work on something together, that is not only special to his son but is crucial and will have a life altering effect on the entire world.

At that very moment, Felix had a flashback, remembering a project he had worked on with Manny a few years ago, so he couldn't wait to get back to work to pull up those specific files.

This way at least he'll already have the information available for Jedi and Nine.

Jedi and Nine Meet with Felix

It was in Felix's DNA to be organized so it didn't take him long to find the project that he had worked on with Manny.

He couldn't believe that he forgot about this specific project, but it was understandable because at the time when the two of them worked on it together, life was still perfect, and once the world became so chaotic, Felix had other things on his mind and totally forgot about that project.

So when Jedi and Nine finally called saying they had something important that they wanted to discuss with him, Felix took this opportunity to tell them about his meeting with Archie, and he was ready to discuss his findings with them but not over the phone.

This was the day they all had agreed to meet, and Felix was more excited than when his son went to the garden of Eden to implement *The Plan*. This was not only exciting but equally as important because this information will bring a type of peace that the entire world desperately needed.

Everyone hugged one another with a different type of hug than before. Before, it was an expectant type of hug, the one you gave out of habit. These hugs today were tighter, and everyone hugged everyone longer than usual. The type of hug, if hugs could speak, would say, "We now have hope in this bleak world."

Once everyone finished hugging, Felix sat down facing both Nine and Jedi so he could see their expressions once he told them his news. He first started off by telling them how proud he was of the two of them and how much their research meant not only to Archie but to the entire world.

At this last statement, Jedi and Nine looked across to one another with that smile that implied "We know how this research brought a light into our dark world," but they let Felix continue.

"I know that you were only researching what Archie asked you to look for in the 'Book of the Law' and in your spare time Nine, you dug even deeper into the book and you found out something that could change the world," said Felix. Felix continued on without skipping a beat: "You discovered that God knew that man would eventually mess up by eating the fruit, which would cause sin to enter the world, which would separate man from God, so He created a way to continue to have a relationship with man, and that would require a sacrifice. You, my dear Nine, discovered that our 'savior' is walking around here on earth now, and both of you would like to speak to me about helping you find Him."

Once they were able to close their mouths, they both quickly said, "Yes."

"I don't want to hold you two in suspense any longer than necessary," Felix said, "but I met the 'savior' a few years ago." He waited a few moments to let it sink it, but to both Jedi and Nine, it seemed like hours.

"Yes, I met Him when He came to me to do research on the genealogy of the 'savior.' I'll make a long story short," continued Felix. "Manny, as He called Himself, was told by His mom when He was old enough to understand His lineage of being the Son of God and what His purpose would be and what it would mean to the world. Instead of accepting this, He read the Book of the Law about various prophets and their prophecy about the Son of God. He took it all in but decided what He read about God and free will, He wouldn't be the 'savior' and also since God is all-knowing, He knew that Manny wouldn't accept this assignment so there must be another person in the world who was the savior.

"Manny decided as an adult He would search for the savior Himself and came to me to help Him with His search. The strange thing is, He worked right here in the company in the IT department. He was a genius with the computers but didn't want to cross any departmental lines, so He asked me to help Him instead. I was getting close to the answer and my computer froze and because it was during the weekend, I called Manny and asked Him to come over to try to fix the problem.

"Wait," he told Jedi and Nine, "it gets even better. I had the worst cramps that I have ever had in my life, and when I came out of the bathroom, the computer was on and repaired, revealing the name of the 'savior', but guess what? Manny was gone too! Yes, not only did I meet the 'savior,' He never came back to work after that, and I found out that He resigned by sending an email to the president of the company."

Gathering of the Future Twelve Disciples

If a stranger had walked in, was introduced to the group of friends that was gathered at Jesus' home and their occupation was given, listening to their conversations and how their different personalities were so different from one another, you would be wondering, "What in the world do they all have in common?"

Jesus decided to wait until the noise level in the room dropped before He spoke to the group of friends who hadn't seen each other prior to when sin had entered the world. Sure, they spoke to each other often over the phone about the mayhem that was occurring throughout the world, but it wasn't the same as when it was pre-sin. They took turns meeting on a regular basis in one another's home.

It was during those times when they talked about their jobs, possibility of new relationships, but the topic that they all found the most exciting was talking about "The Book of the Law."

They were fascinated about what the prophets had written about the time when the presence of God would no longer be sensed because sin had entered the world and separated man from God and how a "savior" would come to bring salvation, hope, and joy along with having a relationship with Him again.

So when their friend Manny called and said it was very important for them to meet because He had some exciting news about "The Book" and "the savior" and it was too important to wait any longer, they had all rearranged their schedules to meet as a group as soon as possible.

The group of friends consisted of four women and eight men. Their personalities ranged from shy and introverted to out-of-the-box loud and controlling.

DJ, as he liked to called, was a photographer. He was one of the shy ones in the group, and needless to say, he enjoyed nature and animals. The pictures he took were so breathtaking, it created opportunities for people to ask him about them, which then allowed DJ to come out of his shell even for a moment. Like a camera, DJ had a photogenic memory, and when he wasn't found taking pictures, he could be found with some type of tool in his had to draw with. Pen, pencil, crayons, or paint—to DJ, it didn't matter.

Chef Harper, as she enjoyed being called by everyone with the exception of her family and close friends, and at times, depending on her mood, even to them, she wouldn't respond to Harper until they put "chef" in front of it. It wasn't that she was conceited or stuck-up or anything like that, it was only because she worked in a profession where the majority of the well-known chefs were men, and she had to constantly be on her toes to prove herself.

In her kitchen, she demanded perfection but with compassion toward her staff, whom she treated like family, which made her a great leader, as well as outside her kitchen. She was always told what a great listener she was.

On the other hand, having Brayden in the group was received with mixed feelings. Since his occupation was being a police officer, he felt that it entitled him to have a controlling personality or otherwise people would run over him.

The group enjoyed remembering what Brayden was like before sin entered the world. Not only was he soft-spoken but someone who was happy to bring anyone into the discussion whom he felt had some valuable insight to share but was too shy to speak up. Brayden and Manny shared similar physical appearance, and from a distance, if you saw them together, you couldn't tell them apart.

Logan, the group's scientist. Every time the group got together, quite a few of them felt as if they were under one of Logan's microscope, being studied. He would stare intently at some of them, taking notes. What the group didn't know was while he was participating in the group's discussion and adding valuable insights to what Manny was saying about "the book," Logan was formulating in his mind and on paper how God and science intertwined.

On the other hand, Logan's younger brother Ezra, who is a physician, couldn't be any different than his older brother. Ezra loved being around people, has a great bedside manner to make them feel comfortable, would treat them as human beings to understand them instead of studying them. Ezra's practice increased tremendously once sin entered the world, not because of the need for medical doctors but because of his reputation with people.

Lincoln has a tendency to be a natural leader. In fact, that's exactly what he did before he and his wife felt it would be best if he stayed at home with the kids rather than his wife quit her job. He was the CEO of a cable company, which required him to travel extensively and miss quite a few of his children's outside activities. He and his wife felt that having one income was more important than having two incomes and missing your kids growing up.

It was nice to be out of the house occasionally to meet with his friends to discuss "the book," and it was during these times that he brought the desserts. Yes, though Chef Harper may be a top-notch chef, Lincoln didn't do too bad in the kitchen either, and everyone always looked forward to his treats.

Roby loved using his imagination which probably was the reason he was a successful architect. He thought outside of the box, and his designs reflected that. His designs not only reflected his vivid imagination, but they were also built based on the environment.

When a building was being built in an area that was known for being hot and humid or extremely cold, the majority of the time, Roby would use natural materials that would keep the building's temperature at a comfortable level without using much electricity or gas. This way he would be conserving the earth's precious natural resources. You could pull him out of his shell by playing games that involved blocks. Roby was still a kid at heart.

His brother Andre', who everyone called Dre', growing up did everything his older brother did. When you saw Roby, not far behind him, you saw Dre'. That was until he discovered that he didn't like being confined to being inside. He discovered his passion for sports during school.

Unlike other student athletics, Dre' didn't want to concentrate on one sport because it seemed like whatever sport he tried out for, he excelled, but he listened to the advice from his parents and concentrated on basketball. It was his outgoing personality that drew people to him. He went on to play college basketball and on to become a professional basketball player.

There are always a few in a group that had to be pulled into a discussion, and when they are, they have valuable information to share. That would be Maya who is a teacher and Aaliyah whose occupation is a graphic designer.

Maya and Aaliyah had the same sweet unassuming personalities until you had them in a conversation regarding an issue that they were passionate about, then you witnessed a different side of them. It was their sweet spirit that also drew people to them, which would be helpful in Jesus' ministry.

Even though Aaliyah was the younger sister of Roby and Dre', she wasn't treated any different in this group of twelve.

Magnus' parents knew that he was destined to be a person whom people respected from the way he carried himself around others as a young adult, but it wasn't until sin entered the world, and lawyers would be needed to defend people based on "the law," which seemed to be a natural change of occupation for Magnus. To change his occupation from being a highly respected businessman to being a lawyer, he naturally questioned and doubted almost everything that was told to him and he wanted to be shown proof, which helped him to be successful.

The twelfth disciple was Kaylee. Kaylee was a writer who loved writing about mysteries. She was the entertainer for the group once they finished discussing "the book" for the night. She would tell the group a story which she made up and have them hanging on to every word that she said, which was frustrating to them because she wouldn't end the story. Instead she would leave the group in suspense until the next time they met.

Yes, this was an eclectic group of people, and they were going to be asked by Jesus to be His disciples.

Jesus Explains Who He Is

Once the room had quieted down, Jesus stepped into the center of the room where everyone was gathered so that He could make eye contact with everyone.

In His friends' eyes, He was still Manny.

Since God showed Him whom to select, He had no doubt that this eclectic group of friends were to be His disciples; however, the human side of Him wondered how they were going to react to the news that He was going to share with them.

The moment Jesus finished explaining all that He had share, how He was told from a young boy who He really was, continuing and enjoying learning about "The Book of the Law," He even shared the part about Him having an expert to trace the lineage for the tribe of Judah to determine if there was another person who might be "the savior" because at the time He choose not to accept His mantel of being "the savior," and since He knew that God gave everyone free will to choose, there had to be someone else in His family line.

He further explained how He went to speak to His cousin Jonny, whom they knew, and to the prophet Jeremiah for some answers about "the savior."

"I always felt they both knew exactly who I was, but they knew in order for it to be more meaningful to Me, that I had to discover the truth on My own and in My own time, and they were right," Jesus said.

Jesus knew that with this curious group of friends that He could only tell a portion of the story, so He ended with how He asked Mr. Jamison, who was an expert on tracing family's lineage from the time of Adam and Eve to present time, to help Him trace the tribe of Judah, starting with David down to present time.

Neither did He leave out the part that He was the one who saw the proof of who He was staring back at Him on Mr. Jamison's computer, when Mr. Jamison had called Him to try to fix a problem on the computer because the computer had frozen, and it being a Saturday, Mr. Jamison had no other choice but to call Him and while Mr. Jamison was using the restroom, the problem with computer seemed to correct itself!

Jesus could see it in all of His friends' eyes. Shock, in awe, admiration, confusion, even signs of hope that they had lost when sin had entered the world were just a few adjectives that could be used.

Jesus had sensed by the look on everyone's faces, and because He didn't want to overwhelm His friends, this was enough information for one day and ended it with a prayer.

"Father God, I thank You for placing this group of people in My life. I pray that You would touch each and everyone's heart, open it to the possibility of what You want to accomplish through each one of them, speak to them in a way that they know without a doubt that it's You, and Father God, prepare their hearts to do Your will." And Jesus ended with "amen."

The group, having a lighter heart, left but not without committing to meet again the following week.

Jesus Sees Jonny Again

The next person Jesus wanted to see again was His cousin Jonny. He couldn't wait to see the expression on Jonny's face when He would tell him about the latest information.

The last time Jesus saw His cousin was when He shared with Jonny that He chose not to accept the responsibility of being the savior and felt that God had a plan B, and He was on a mission to search for answers regarding who "the savior" was before sin had entered the world.

This was a two-fold visit for Jesus. One, to catch up with one another, and two, Jesus wanted to ask Jonny to baptize Him.

Once sin had entered the world, Jesus knew that Jonny began his ministry, which was going around the country teaching and preaching the good news about "the savior," repentance, and also for people to be baptized.

People were willing to listen to Jonny's message, and many hearts were turned and understood that by being baptized that it is a public showing to show those who were around by being submerged into the water that you went under as one who was part of a sinning world who had repented for the sin they did, and when they came up, it would be as a new person who wanted to obey God and have a personal relationship with Him.

Some of these people were the ones who remembered what it was like to have a personal relationship with God before sin entered the world, and the others were ones who felt that tugging on their heart once they heard Jonny's message.

Now of course, Jonny also knew that his message would not be received on a positive note by everyone. His hardest group to convince was "the religious group," the Xians. These were the ones that

God had forewarned him about who would be causing trouble for him since they too had studied "The Book," and they felt that they were the experts, enjoyed judging others, and didn't care for what Jonny was teaching and preaching.

Jesus caught Jonny up on everything that had happened to Him by telling him exactly what He had shared with His group of friends and also how He wanted His friends to represent Himself.

Once Jesus finished sharing the story, He wasted no time in telling Jonny why He was there. "Look, Jonny, I understand now why you couldn't tell Me what I was looking for when we last met," Jesus started saying, "and now I would like for You to baptize Me."

"Wait a minute, Manny, I mean, Jesus," said Jonny, shocked by what he had heard. "Why do You want me to baptize You? You have no sin to repent for? For goodness sake, You are the Son of God! You are the person that I have been preaching and teaching about to prepare people's heart for until You came."

Jonny had trouble calming himself down once he realized how he was speaking to the Son of God. This was different than when they met before because then, Jesus hadn't accepted who He was.

Jesus had to contain the laughter He was feeling inside, seeing the discomfort He was causing His poor cousin.

"Yes, I know that, Jonny, but when I start My ministry, I want people to also know that because I am God in human flesh, that I am able to have the same experiences that they have in life. I came so that they would have an everlasting life with My Father.

"What a better way to demonstrate this by being baptized in the same matter as all those folks did?" He ended with, "And there is no one else that I would love to share this experience with. Remember the story that our mothers told when we first met each other while we were still in our mother's womb?"

What other answer could Jonny say but "yes"?

Jonny Baptizes Jesus

By this time, Jonny learned to use the internet for his benefit after he had someone he trusted create a website for his ministry, sharing the same information he was sharing in public and also on his website at times gave information of where he would be speaking.

It was during those times that when he spoke, he received so much joy in sharing about the love of God, he knew he wouldn't have chosen to be anywhere else.

This particular day, when the gathering of people was larger than normal. Jonny just took it in stride. He felt that nothing but good could come out of this event when he baptized Jesus.

Was Jonny ever correct. As he was bringing Jesus up after being submerged in the water, the few clouds that were over everyone's heads had parted, and Jesus saw the Spirit of God descending like a dove above His head as a voice spoke, and people recognized it as being the voice of God, who said, "This is My beloved Son, in whom I am well pleased."

Isn't it just like God to orchestrate having a large crowd to witness this special event, who thought they were coming to hear Jonny's preaching and teaching and not to physically hear from God?

Once God said what He said, people were stunned into silence until Jonny's loud "Praise the Lord!" broke the crowd's silence.

People loved to talk, and this time it was a good thing. This event spread by both word of mouth and through the internet. What the people did not know what had occurred during this event was that the spirit of God anointed Jesus for His own ministry.

The Church

The attendance at both Pastors Jerry and Don's churches had increased since sin had entered the world along with other churches that they had to add multiple services on Sunday and also services during the week.

Both pastors not only follow Jonny's website but were in attendance when Jonny baptized Jesus.

Not only were the pastors there in attendance to witness this event, Pastors Don and Jerry heard from God a few Sundays prior to this event, who told them to invite their entire congregation.

As all the churches were going through a difficult time, their churches had some people who were skeptical, and they were grateful that they each had enough people signed up to fill seven buses. They weren't disappointed that more didn't show up because they both knew that God was in charge, and whatever was going to happen that day, it was going to change the lives of everyone who attended.

What they witnessed was a miracle. Not only did they hear a message regarding repentance, which they both planned on teaching to their congregations for a few months or until they felt it was time to move on to another subject, but they witnessed the world's Savior being baptized when they heard the voice of God saying that He was proud of His Son!

That night both pastors went to their perspective blogs to share what they had experienced, and they weren't surprised at how many people responded in a positive way. They encouraged everyone who wanted to know more to go to Jonny's website.

For the next few months, the message of repentance and baptismal was shared throughout the world. People were eager to have peace in their lives again. This didn't make the devil and his minions happy at all.

Jedi and Nine Search for Jesus

Once Felix shared the information about Jesus, they also used the internet for their benefit.

After trying not to be discouraged and not give up, Jedi and Nine looked at each other and said, "What are we missing here? What keywords should we be using?"

Nine asked Jedi, "When we met with Isaiah, do you remember what he said about the savior? That He would be known as the Son of God. Let's look up 'Son of God,'" Nine said.

"Son of God" was a hit!

In order to search the internet faster, they both used their own computers and didn't say anything to each other until they felt they had found something significant.

Jedi spoke first. "Nine, I might have found something. It says here that this Jonny person has a ministry, and he goes around preaching and teaching about the good news, which I remember Isaiah also saying. Anyway, it says in this particular article that when he was sharing his message, that this man came up to be baptized, and when He came up from the water, the crowd heard the voice of God who said, 'This is My beloved Son, in whom I am well pleased.'"

"Well, Nine?" Jedi asked.

"I think it's time to plan a road trip," said Nine.

"That was my first reaction too, but," continued Jedi, "because of our part in creating this confusing world, and I'm not bringing this up to hurt your feelings, Nine, I think we should first reach out to this Jonny person, explain exactly who we are, and see if he can arrange to have us meet with Jesus."

"You're right, Jedi," said Nine.

With that being said, this time working on one computer, they went back to Jonny's website to get additional information.

Jonny's website was different than most websites. His didn't advertise a phone number to contact him, and the only way to see him was in person. So that's exactly what they did.

Every day for a few weeks, they took the time to read what was being said on Jonny's website. Not only was all the information useful, it gave them a sense of peace, and they weren't even yet in his presence.

What seemed strange to both of them was after the story about Jesus being baptized by Jonny was on the internet, nothing else was said about Jesus. It was as if He had dropped out of sight.

Nine and Jedi would soon learn that Jesus was busy organizing His own ministry.

Jesus Explains His Ministry
to His Disciples

"Well, My friends," Jesus started, "thank you for taking time out of your busy schedules to meet with Me again.

"During this time, I will explain to you what our ministry will be about.

"As we had read in 'The Book' that God knew there was going to be a time in history that His presence would no longer be felt on the earth once sin entered the world, and because He knew this, He would have a plan to redeem people from their sins that would draw them close to Him again."

"I, My friends, am the plan for redemption, and the Holy Spirit, which is God's power in action will be with Me, as you are all aware that I now go by Jesus, and I'm not saying this to sound uppity or anything, but those who follow Me will be called Christians because of My official title 'Jesus Christ, the Son of God.'

We are to go around the country to explain the simple truth, similar to what My cousin Jonny has been saying.

God wants to have a relationship again with the people, and because sin and God can't exist together, the people need to recognize in their hearts that they have sinned, need to repent in order to have a personal relationship with God, also believe that I am the Son of God. People have been hurting since sin entered, and I have come to seek and save those who are lost. If their hearts are in the right place, by doing these things, they will live forever in heaven with God and saving them from an eternal life in hell."

"Our message will be about love. The type of love that God has for everyone, and He doesn't want to see anyone go to hell. The type of love that a father has for his son. He also wants to be known to them as Father God. They must be born again. When they accept this action, their hearts will be changed to want to do the right thing. Will this stop them from sinning? Of course not, once they recognized that they sinned, all they need to do is stop what they are doing right away, admit the sin that they committed, repent, and ask God for forgiveness."

"Let's do this, friends. Since we are all here now, let's all go together to hear Jonny's message on the gospel. We will meet again next week and at that time if you have any additional questions that I may answer and I also hope to hear your answers about being a part of My ministry."

Jedi and Nine Hear Jonny's Message

J edi and Nine found the location of where Jonny was going to delivery his message from his website. They both assumed that it would be at some fancy auditorium with surround sound and the latest bells and whistles in the electronic world. The directions on the website led them to an area where the only way you could gain access was by parking your car and walking a quarter of a mile away.

The area had a similar resemblance to the garden of Eden, which startled them. The grass was lush and soft enough for them to sit down, which was nice because they didn't bring any chairs or a blanket to sit on, and they were surrounded by mountains.

Once they found a place to sit among the hundreds who were also there, Jedi leaned over to Nine and whispered, "If he only speaks at places similar to this, and we are able to speak to him today, how would you feel about me suggesting to him that he puts on his website about people bringing chairs or blankets?"

Before Nine could answer Jedi's question, Jonny began to speak.

Since they didn't see any equipment set up, they were amazed of the natural acoustics that the mountains provided in this intimate setting.

His message started off the way it normally goes regarding repentance, and he was there to prepare the people to open up their hearts to hear from Jesus, whom by this time was known to some as the Son of God.

The message about repentance was so clear that you had to be deaf to miss it.

He told his audience that repentance wasn't a ritual or some sort of sacrifice but an action, an actual turning of one's heart and life from sin to God's way of life, and he connected this message with being baptized in water, which represents one acknowledging that they had sinned and seeking cleansing of their souls and forgiveness.

As he ended his teaching and began inviting people to be baptized, Nine turned around to see how Jedi had reacted to this invitation. Jedi was already on his feet with his hand gesturing to Nine to help her up.

As they walked hand in hand toward Jonny and the body of water to be baptized in, no words were necessary to be said between the two of them. They knew without a doubt this was something that they both wanted and needed—a cleansing of their souls.

Once they were near the front of the line to be baptized, a man approached them and gently pulled them a few feet away from the crowd and said to them, "Jedi and Nine, God wanted Me to tell you that He feels the pain that you both have been in since that time in the garden of Eden. He knows your hearts and wants to comfort you both and will give you peace and a hope, along with Him telling you that your sins will been forgiven and that He'll never forsake you."

"Who are You?" stammered Nine. "And how do You know our names?'

"My name is Jesus" was the reply.

Nine and Jedi's Personal Encounter with Jesus

"And I would like to baptize you both," He said. They were both surprised and humbled at His request, to which they both said together, "Yes."

As they walked together to the body of water where they were to be baptized, Jesus took this opportunity to get to know them a little better.

"Nine and Jedi," He began, "do you both believe that I am the Son of God? I know that you're both very intelligent, or how else would you have been able to enter My garden? But what I mean is, in your heart, do you believe that I am the Son of God?"

They both nodded their heads "yes," since it seemed as if their voices had left them.

"My Father, whom by the way would love for you to call Him that, would like for you both to know that He is not angry with either one of you. Nothing takes Him by surprise, and I mean nothing, which includes your visit to the garden.

"By being baptized and saying that you accept by faith that I am the Son of God, you are accepting God's way to live for your lives."

Jesus baptized Jedi first, as Nine who stood on the edge of the pond, as Jedi was being led into the water by Jesus to be baptized. Before Jesus was going to submerge Jedi into the water, He said to him, "Jedi, God wants you to know that He is so proud of you and what you have accomplished since sin entered the world and would appreciate it if from now you would go by your given name of 'Jedidiah.' In case you didn't know, it means 'friend of God.'"

Since his voice hadn't yet returned, he again nodded "yes," and at that time, Jedidiah was baptized by the Son of God.

****

"Am I glowing?" were the first words that was spoken by Nine.

"Huh?" was Jedidiah's reply, whose voice finally returned.

"I feel as if I can bring light into a dark room, and the weight that I had been carrying since the time in the garden has finally been lifted," she said.

Nine had been carrying on and on since they've gotten into the car and started heading home that she realized Jedi hadn't said anything since the baptismal.

"Jedi," she softly said as she leaned over to touch his arm.

"About you calling me Jedi," he said, "before Jesus baptized me, He told me that God was proud of everything that I had done and would like for me to start going by my given name, which you know, is Jedidiah."

"Why?" Nine asked, somewhat shocked until she heard that Jedidiah's name meant "friend of God."

"And to answer your question," replied Jedidiah, "yes, I feel the same way you do, knowing that God has forgiven me, He's not angry, and He's given me peace. What more can I ask for?"

Nine chimed in to say, "You know that this is not just the beginning of a new way of life for us?" Before Jedidiah could say anything, Nine continued, "I read on one of Jonny's website how important it is for those who have been recently baptized to continue to grow by going to a church whose pastor or teacher has been baptized so we can all be taught the same message that Jonny is teaching. It's also important for us to tell those that we love and care about this message because God doesn't want anyone to go to hell." At that point, Nine stopped talking and waited to hear what Jedidiah had to say.

Jedidiah's response was simply "I agree."

Jesus' Ministry

Jesus knew by taking His friends to hear what Jonny had to say about repentance and the gospel would open their hearts and minds to also what He had to share.

He had explained to them that His and their ministry was to not only teach and preach the truth of the gospel of God but also to heal.

People were dying and didn't know what to expect with their lives; therefore, no one had hope. Everyone seemed lost. Jesus came to seek out those who were lost and try to save them for the kingdom of God. He had to let people know what would happen to their souls once they died. They were either going to "heaven" or "hell," and of course He shared what the difference would be.

Jesus wanted the people to be aware of the love that God has for them and doesn't want anyone to go to "hell" but wants them to live out eternally in His kingdom with Him. People had to first accept Him by faith as the Son of God and repent.

He shared with His disciples that more often than not, He spent time alone praying and speaking with His Father God. What He did during that time was gaining strength from God to complete His mission.

It was important to His ministry that Jesus could relate to what problems people might experience because He too was tempted by the devil. He didn't stand around and argue with the devil, He just stood on the words of what God said about each situation that the devil threw at Him, and the devil left Him alone.

Jesus also shared with the disciples that they would come up against many oppositions.

For the next three years, Jesus and His disciples went around the country sharing the gospel of the kingdom of God. The crowds that He spoke to grew larger and larger. They could sense His compassion when speaking. When He made eye contact with you, you felt like you were the only one He was speaking to.

There were times when people who were sick with illnesses or diseases came to hear Him speak and He healed them all of their diseases and because Jesus' events were also being shared on the internet, parents would bring their babies who were born either blind, deaf, cripple, or with some type of aliment, and Jesus would heal them all. He wouldn't turn anyone away without first healing them.

Seeing people and babies being healed opened up their hearts, and once their hearts were opened, they would be more open to hear what Jesus had to say about His teachings.

Jesus preferred the same natural outdoor settings as His cousin Jonny did with natural acoustics for His gatherings. It did not matter how large the crowd was, everyone heard what Jesus was saying.

During one of these gatherings, the day started off as a beautiful day, with enough cloud covering to give a small breeze on a sunny day, and out of nowhere, a torrential rainstorm came down which cause people to start running for cover.

All of a sudden, everyone heard Jesus speak with authority and told the wind and the rain, "Peace be still!" and both the rain and the wind ceased and there was a calmness with the weather as well as with the group of people.

"*Who can control the weather with just their voice?*" were the thoughts of everyone who saw this of miraculous feat of Jesus.

His disciples remembered at that moment how Jesus explained to them that the Holy Spirit, who is with Jesus, is God's power in action!

The torrential wind and rain storm and how Jesus told them both to be still came at the perfect opportunity as Jesus had just shared with this group that He is the Son of God. What better way to vindicate who He says He is by showing He has control over nature!

Not everyone was happy with Jesus. The same group of people who had called the prophet Jeremiah "the weeping prophet" had grown only in size but not with knowledge.

There was that other group of religious people who weren't rabbis but called themselves "Xians." They were teachers who also knew about God through "studying 'The Book of the Law'" but didn't believe that Jesus was the Son of God.

The more Jesus talked about the love that God has for His people, forgiveness, and repentance, the more annoyed and outraged the Xians became.

The Xians were angry at Jesus for a number of reasons. Jesus called them out and told them that it was wrong for them to oppress others and to treat them unfairly. Not only did they not want to believe His claim of being the Son of God, who was sent into the world to save people from their sins, they didn't want to change their ways, much less repent.

When the Xians tried to taunt Jesus, He again called them out for their hypocrisy. They didn't hate Jesus for not only calling them out but because He threatened their security, prestigious status, and income. They felt Jesus had a lack of respect for religious traditions, and He was going to ruin everything they had worked so hard for.

The more attention Jesus received only created more hatred and jealousy, and it was both of these feelings combined, which caused the Xians to want Jesus dead.

Jesus Explains His Death
to the Disciples

Jesus knew that His time on earth was drawing near, and it was time to talk with His disciples about His death. It wasn't going to be an easy conversation to have, and just as He always did, He first went to pray to His Father about the words that He should say.

The sense in the atmosphere when His disciples met with Him for Him to discuss His death was different this time than any other times before. It wasn't an unpleasant sense in the atmosphere, just different. Jesus as always, opened up with a prayer.

"Father God," He began, "I truly thank You for bringing these people into My life, who I not only call 'friends' but My 'disciples'. I pray that You touch each and every one of their hearts in a way that they know that it's You, for them to desire more of You in their lives and to accept what I am about to share with them. Amen," Jesus ended.

"In the beginning, when I first brought you all together and to share with you, who I was and what My responsibility to the world was to bring and share the good news of salvation. That comes at a price. The price is My death." Jesus said it just so matter-of-factly that it took a while for it to register with His disciples.

They all had a look of disbelief on their faces.

Chef Harper was the first one to speak. "Umm, can I make anyone something to eat?" This was her way to leave an uncomfortable situation that she had no control over.

Jesus went over to Harper, placed an arm around her, and softly said, "Harper, maybe later you can make us something delicious to eat, but right now this is so important that I want everyone to hear it at the same time."

So as Harper sat back down with her friends, Jesus continued to speak. "This is not a sad occasion, friends," Jesus started, "I was born to die, just as every one of you will die. The only difference will be that I was born to die to pay for the sins of mankind."

"Ever since sin entered the world, you all felt a separation from God. That's because God can't be where sin is, and He requires a payment or sacrifice if you will, for the price of sin. That's where I come in because I am the Son of God, and I have never sinned, I am willing to take on all the sins of the world that happened in the past, present, and future. In order to do this, it was written in 'The Book' that I must die a violent death, but the good news is in order for people to know that I am who I said I am, the Son of God, I will rise up from the dead on the third day."

"I must do this," Jesus said, "not only to be a sacrifice for mankind but so the Holy Spirit will come upon everyone who becomes a believer."

"If you noticed that I can only be in one place at a time, and God is everywhere, this is the same with the Holy Spirit. The Holy Spirit can be everywhere. The Holy Spirit that will raise Me from the dead will also be in you. What miracles you saw Me do, you will do greater things because the Holy Spirit will live in you, but in order for this to happen, I must die for you to use the name of Jesus, and to tell you the truth, it is to your advantage that I do go away, for if I don't go away, the Holy Spirit will not come to you, but if I leave, I will send the Holy Spirit to you." Jesus also said, "All things that the Father has are Mine."

"I know your hearts are heavy with what I have just told you about Me dying, but please believe Me when I say I will see you again and your heart will rejoice and that your joy, no one can take from you."

To this announcement, the disciples did not understand what Jesus meant and were afraid to ask Him about it. It was understandable that no one was hungry after Jesus dropped this bombshell on them, so Jesus ended the evening with a prayer.

"Father God, again I thank You for this group of friends whom You have placed in My life for a specific reason. I know that they are feeling confused and have many questions to ask. I pray that as they go to sleep tonight that their minds do not become agitated with the things they learned tonight but surround them with Your peace. Father God, they will need Your strength along with the Holy Spirit in order to endure what is coming within the next couple of months. Amen."

As Jesus ended His prayer, the group of friends left in a total different mood as when they arrived.

Once outside the home, the group of friends decided to meet again, this time without Jesus, so they can try to comprehend what was just said.

Xians Devise a Plan to Kill Jesus

The Xians have not been a happy group of people since Jesus came onto the scene with His ministry.

They felt it was bad enough to have this Jonny person around preaching the Word of God in a way that brought hope to an otherwise hopeless world, but they didn't feel threatened with Jonny the way they felt threatened with Jesus, so something had to be done.

It was during one of their many conversations about Jesus when someone had said, "Wouldn't it be great to be rid of both Jesus and Jonny at the same time?"

"How?" was the next question.

The devil and his minions love to infiltrate a group such as the Xians, who could easily be manipulated.

What the group wasn't aware of was that one of their own, Jahi, had been trying to find a way to became the head of the Xians, and what a better way to gain popularity with the group than to bring the demise of Jesus?

So he took it upon himself to infiltrate Jesus' group of disciples by getting to know Harper better at her restaurant, who eventually invited Jahi to one of their meetings. He often went to their meetings, and he even participated with the discussions with the disciples.

As interesting as the meetings might have been and being drawn into the conversations with the disciples more than once about the subject of salvation, there was a voice in his head that kept saying, "You're here to see how you can bring down Jesus and not to be saved and become one of them, so focus on your agenda."

Jahi's name means "dignified," but somehow being in this group of Xians for only a year and what he was planning to accomplish proves that he did not live up to his name.

It was during one of the meetings with the disciples that Jahi noticed the close resemblance to both Jesus and Brayden, and just to make sure he wasn't the only one who thought so, he pulled Lincoln aside and asked him innocently, "Is it my imagination or could Jesus and Brayden pass for brothers?"

Lincoln chuckled and replied, "Funny that you should ask that question, but you wouldn't believe how many times that Brayden have been out with us, without Jesus, and from a distance, people have yelled, 'Jesus, Jesus,' and when they came face to face with Brayden, they realized that it wasn't Jesus."

Jahi's mind started racing with the most devious plan he could come up with once Lincoln made this statement.

Let me try to convince Brayden to kill Jonny for money and how we plan to frame Jesus for the killing, he was thinking to himself. *He will somehow get Jonny away from his group by sending him an email saying it's from Jesus, asking to meet. The meeting needs to take place far enough away from security cameras where at an angle it looks like Jesus but not close enough to tell that it wasn't Jesus. I can have a few members of our group be in the area to be witnesses to the meeting. Brayden will start a heated argument with Jonny and kill him with a knife.*

The last idea Jahi thought about would be the argument for the prosecutor—that Jonny was jealous of Jesus' ministry, and there could only be one true ministry.

Jahi, from what he gathered from interacting with the disciples, Jesus loved being by Himself praying, and if He wasn't in meetings or anywhere around, the majority of the times, He was in a secluded place in prayer.

Jahi was proud of his plan and couldn't wait to tell the others. What Jahi didn't realize that he was being used by the devil to further his agenda.

The Disciples Meet without Jesus

The group of disciples couldn't wait to meet so that they could discuss amongst themselves what Jesus had told them about Him dying and without having Him around.

Logan was the first one to speak his mind. "I don't know about you guys, but did it make sense to you what Jesus had said about Him dying and then will come back to life after three days? I'm a scientist and I'm telling you that's impossible!" he ended.

"Well, we all can't forget that we have witnessed the miracles that He performed," interrupted Kaylee, "how He has healed everyone who came to see Him, no matter how severely ill they were, so we know by witnessing these events, all things are possible with Him."

"The way He spoke to the wind and rain that day, and He told them to be quiet."

"We believe that He is the Son of God, so we just need to believe by faith that He will do what He says," said Kaylee.

"Should I design an elaborate place to put His body?" asked Roby.

"What good would that do, Roby?" asked his brother Andre, who continued with, "if He said He'll be raised up in three days."

"I may not want to believe what Jesus said about Him dying, but at least I want Him to have the best resting place for the time that He has on the earth," explained Roby.

"That brings up another question," asked Ezra, "do we know when this will all take place, sooner rather than later?"

Everyone started formulating thoughts in their own heads.

How will he die? thought DJ, *and should I start taking more pictures now to document His ministry since we don't know when it will end?* This is the line of thought mostly everyone had about the death of Jesus.

Kaylee thought to herself how she should start writing down notes now of everything that has and will take place. Sure, she might have a great memory, but being around Jesus and documenting His life and ministry was too of an important event in history to leave to memory.

Maya felt she had the perfect audience with her students to talk about Jesus, and even if it wasn't an approved subject to teach, this wasn't teaching. She was only doing what Jesus wanted her to do. Talk about the good news.

Aaliyah had been sketching and using her abilities as a graphic designer during this time and had created an extensive portfolio of Jesus, His healings, and teachings, along with the disciples, which she thought would be a great way to honor Him.

The rest of the disciples didn't want to believe what Jesus had told them, so they remained in a state of denial—with the exception of Brayden. He felt turmoil within his soul, and he couldn't explain it to anyone because he didn't understand it himself.

The Death of Jonny

I t didn't take long for Jahi to convince the group of Xians regarding his plan to have Brayden kill Jonny and frame Jesus for his death because they felt that it was the perfect plan and this way they wouldn't have any blood on their hands.

Brayden, on the other hand, took longer to be convinced by Jahi to take on this heinous act.

Because the group of disciples were used to having Jahi around, it was during one of their meetings when they spoke about what Jesus had recently shared with them about His impending death.

Jahi used this discussion to his benefit when he approached Brayden with this idea.

He met with Brayden alone in a secluded place and told him of his plan. He asked Brayden if he believed Jesus when He said that He was going to die but be raised up in three days.

When Brayden responded with a "yes," Jahi knew at that moment that he had him. "Now listen very carefully, with what I'm about to explain to you," started Jahi. "Since you believe what Jesus said about Himself dying and being raised up in three days, how would you like to be a part of His plan and make money doing it?"

The moment Jahi mentioned money, Brayden sat up straighter and began to listen more intently, to which he told Jahi, "Tell me more."

So Jahi began to explain the plan to Brayden. "When I was in a few meetings with you and the other disciples, I noticed a strong resemblance between you and Jesus, and once I confirmed this with Lincoln who said that on occasions people have thought that you were Jesus, so I actually thought we could use this resemblance to our benefit.

147

"We want you to kill Jesus' cousin Jonny," Jahi said without any emotion in his voice.

"Whoa, wait a minute!" Brayden almost shouted, putting his hands out in front of him as to say, "Stay away from me," but he continued with, "You didn't say this involved me killing anyone, let alone Jesus' cousin Jonny, but before I say 'no,' I'm curious to hear how you plan on pulling this off."

"Well, Brayden," began Jahi, "to be honest with you, since I've already shared this part of the plan with you, the only choice you have at this moment is to go along with the plan, or we will kill you too."

We always have choices, but the mention of Brayden possible being killed and the excitement of having all that money—well, money won over any moral dilemmas that Brayden might have had.

Once Jahi explained the plan in depth to Brayden, Brayden felt that the plan was foolproof and said "yes." It didn't even matter to Brayden why they would want to kill Jonny, only that he would be getting paid!

****

The death of Jonny was breaking news around the world! Every television and radio station had interrupted their regularly scheduled programs to bring this news throughout the world. Not only had Jonny died, but he had been murdered!

His disciples couldn't be contained and demanded answers from the authorities.

Jesus took this opportunity to pray about what just had happened to Jonny and again with His disciples to speak to them about His impending death.

They all felt in their souls, since Jonny had just recently been killed, and Jesus spoke about His impending death, that there was a religious serial fanatic out there also seeking to harm Jesus. So again, no one asked Jesus any questions, just listened.

Jonny's Disciples Demanding Answers

The police department knew because of the status of Jonny, that this was to be considered a high-profile case which needed to be solved sooner rather than later.

Destiny, the chief of police, put her best detectives on the case and said in no uncertain term that they would not stop their investigation until they had apprehended the person or persons that were involved in this heinous crime.

This was the first murder that had taken place since sin had entered the world, and the world was reeling.

Thank goodness for security cameras, thought Detectives Rosales and Anderson, *but they couldn't believe what they saw.*

The only camera that was able to capture the attack on Jonny was at a distance and something was wrong with the zoom-in function and even with the best techies that the police department had, they couldn't get the zoom-in function to work, so the detectives could only rely on what they saw. They saw Jesus attacking Jonny!

Rosales was the first one who found his voice. "This can't be, Anderson," he said to his partner. "Everything we've been told or have seen about Jesus is Him speaking on love and the love of God. There isn't an evil bone in His body."

"I agree with you," answered Anderson, "but we can't deny what's right in front of us in black and white."

"I'll tell you what," continued Anderson, "let's check out more security footage from other cameras in the same area around the same time that Jonny was attacked to see if there were any other witnesses around."

"Sounds like a plan," replied Rosales.

Between the two of them working, it didn't take them long to discover that a couple of blocks down, there was a group of three men, standing around talking.

Fortunately, the zoom-in function on this security camera in this specific area was working, so all they had to do was to identify who the three men were and to call them in for questioning.

Of course these three men were planted there from the Xians group to help substantiate what the detectives think they saw on the security camera.

The three men had already discussed what their lie would be when questioned. They even went as far as having their testimony written out for them, committed to memory, also were questioned individually by the other members of the Xians to ensure their stories matched up with each other and didn't change.

The next day, when the detectives were given the approval to publicly show the three men's faces on television and also on the internet to ask the public's help to identify the men for questioning regarding the death of Jonny, the three men showed up to the police station before the day was even over.

These three men were chosen by their group of fellow Xians because of their personalities and their ability to make anyone believe anything that they said, and of course, when the Xians said they would throw in extra money, well, this just made them want to perform that much better.

Both Rosales and Anderson couldn't believe their luck when these three men came to the police station so fast in response to the media outreach that they didn't have a chance to set up the individually waiting rooms, so they could be interviewed one at a time.

Once the rooms were set up, Rosales and Anderson took the first two, and Rosales questioned the last one. The detectives each had papers with the exact same questions written on them that they were to ask their witnesses, and all their responses were exactly the same.

"They had just finished eating dinner at the Sea Salt Restaurant around eight-ish and decided to walk off their dinner before returning to their cars."

"When they past by Jonny and Jesus speaking to each other in heated voices, they didn't think anything of it because the entire world knew that they were cousins."

"Being human, the three of them slowed down their steps to see if they could hear more of what the argument was about."

"Jonny was upset that Jesus' ministry was taking off better than his was and told Jesus that He needed to back down and have less public appearances where teachings and miracles were taken place so Jonny's ministry could continue to flourish."

"We were shocked when we heard Jesus answer, 'I guess by you saying this, Jonny, that there is only room for one of us.'"

"We've all seen the face of Jesus on television or on the internet, but we have never seen this look on His face. It was the face of an angry man."

"At this time, we all felt uncomfortable and being intrusive with what we had just heard, so we slowly turned around and left."

"When we read the headlines the next day, we couldn't understand who would want Jonny dead, and until you had showed us the footage of Jesus and Jonny talking, and no one else was around, we assumed the killing took place by someone else once Jesus left Jonny."

Jesus Is Questioned

Once again, the chief of police had an important decision to make once those three witnesses corroborated what everyone in the police department saw on the security camera.

Jesus' case will be even more of a high-profile case than His cousin's Jonny was, Destiny thought to herself.

"We have been hounded with calls from both reporters and Jonny's disciples for answers, and before I go public with what we have discovered, I need to question Jesus about the night in question," Destiny said, still thinking to herself.

The first time that Destiny saw and heard Jesus speak in public was when she had recently broken up with what she thought was the love of her life, and she felt lost. After hearing the compassion in Jesus' voice about salvation, hope, and the love of God that He has for everyone, she did feel that love and gave her life to Jesus and was baptized at the same time.

No one knew that she was a follower of Jesus, and she kept that personal part of her life to herself.

"What a dilemma this is." Destiny sighed as she approached to knock on Jesus' door. As she was raising her hand to knock, Jesus opened the door.

Destiny forgot just how piercing Jesus' eyes were. Not in an uncomfortable way but in a way that He was looking into your soul and knew all about you.

"Hello," Jesus started with. "Haven't we met before?"

Destiny, who is in a career where it is demanded that she cannot ever be at a loss for words, managed to stammer out a "yes."

"Please come in, miss…" asked Jesus.

"Destiny. My name is Destiny," she said, "and I am the city's chief of police."

After sitting down in the living room and saying, "No, thank you" to water when offered by Jesus, Destiny started on the speech that she had been practicing to say to Jesus all the way from her office to His home.

"There is no easy way to say this, Sir," started Destiny.

"Please call me Jesus," He said.

"There is no easy way to say this, Jesus," she started saying again. "We have reviewed the footage on the security camera, and since the zoom-in function on the security camera in that specific area was not working, the department had hoped that there might have been some witnesses in the area that could come forward." At this point, Destiny lowered her voice, and her speech also slowed down.

"We were lucky when my detectives were given the approval to show the public the faces of the three men on television that was on another security camera in the area and also on the internet to ask the public's help to identify the men to help corroborate what we thought we saw on the security camera, and to make a long story short, Jesus, we questioned each of the three men separately, asking them the same questions, and they all had the same exact answer, which was that they saw and heard You and Jonny arguing.

"My next question for You, Jesus, is," Destiny said softly, "where were You on the night in question around eight-fifteen?"

"Praying alone with God," was Jesus' answer.

Destiny was praying for a different answer, one that would include Him being around anyone else. "I am so sorry to say this to You, Sir, but You are under arrest for the murder of Your cousin Jonny." And Destiny asked, "Is there anyone that I can call?"

Jesus was already aware of how His disciples would react to this news, and He thought it would make them feel more comfortable, even if He knew how it was all going to end, that it would be better if He was represented by someone in His group.

"Yes, please, Destiny," Jesus answered. "Would you please call Magnus? He is an attorney and also one of My disciples."

Jesus Arrested

It didn't take long for Magnus to go see Jesus where He was being held, and during the ride to the police department, which seemed as if it took hours which in all actuality it only took fifteen minutes, Magnus' mind was being pulled in different directions with a few questions.

"What was Jesus being arrested for? Should I call the others? How is Jesus doing in jail?" were just the beginning of questions until he saw Jesus.

Destiny decided she would personally take on this case because she had felt a connection to Jesus, so she remained at the jail until Magnus arrived.

"Who's in charge of this place?" yelled Magnus as he was using his "walking with a purpose" stride, entering the jail.

"I am," replied Destiny, knowing who he was from the pictures on the internet.

"Where is Jesus? What is He being held for, and I need to see Him now!" said Magnus, still shouting.

"First of all Magnus, my name is Destiny, and I am the city's chief of police," she said as she ushered Magnus to a small conference room, "and I'll answer all of your questions once I share the facts with you that we have against your client.

Magnus again tried not to get upset by the chief of police's use of the word "client."

"This arrest is in connection with the murder of Jonny, and before you can say anything, please hear my story first."

For the sake of being consistent, she told Magnus exactly what she shared with Jesus regarding the night in question that Jonny was murdered. "When we reviewed the footage from the security camera

154

in the area of where Jonny was murdered that evening, and because the security camera in that area's zoom-in function was not working, the department had hoped that there might have been some witnesses in the area that would come forward." At this point, Destiny again lowered her voice, and her speech also slowed down because she knew how this news must be affecting him.

"Well, we were lucky when my detectives were given the approval to show to the public the three men's faces on television that was on a security camera and also on the internet to ask the public's help to identify the men to help corroborate what we thought we saw on the security camera, and to make a long story short, Magnus, when we questioned each of the three men separately, asking them the same questions, they all had the same exact answer, which was that they saw and heard Jesus and Jonny arguing."

Magnus started murmuring under his breath. He took a deep breath and said very deliberately and slowly, "Destiny, it is a good thing for you that I had stopped cussing when I became a follower of Jesus, otherwise, you might have had to put me in a jail cell next to Jesus until I calmed down."

"I'm happy to hear that too," replied Destiny.

"May I see please the footage from the security camera?" asked Magnus.

"I took the liberty to have it already set up in the next room, so follow me, and we'll look at it together," replied Destiny.

Once Magnus viewed the footage, he understood why witnesses were needed because there wasn't any way to be one hundred percent sure to identify who the person was on the camera.

"Destiny, as Jesus' attorney, I am going to do my due diligence to prove His innocence because both you, me, and the entire world knows that, that Man, whom you have under arrest, isn't capable of killing anyone," Magnus ended, sounding defeated.

"I understand completely how you must feel Magnus, however, my job is to uphold the law and the law states that when we have two or more witnesses for a crime. It must go to court for a decision to be rendered by a jury of His peers," Destiny said in her matter-of-fact voice.

"May I now see my friend?" asked Magnus.

"Of course" was Destiny's answer.

"Destiny, may I ask another favor please?" Magnus asked. "Would you please not publicize His arrest until I have a chance to meet with my group of friends as soon as possible?"

Destiny looked directly into Magnus' eyes and answered, "Yes, of course."

Jesus and Magnus

Magnus didn't know what to expect when he went into the room where Jesus was being held.

His eyes quickly darted around the room to determine if there were any recording devices to tape their conversation. *"You don't know who you can trust now days."* he thought to himself.

He pulled up a chair alongside Jesus, just as friends do when having a normal conversation, even if this conversation was going to be anything but normal.

The look on Jesus' face did not reflect any stress or concern which made Magnus wonder what was going on in His mind.

"Magnus," Jesus started, "as much as I appreciate you being here to defend Me, we both know how this will end."

"But Jesus, I just can't sit by and watch them railroad You into something that everyone knows You didn't do," he said, sounding defeated. "I'm going to prove to the world that You are innocent, if it's the last thing that I do!"

Jesus sat back thinking about the last conversation that He had with His disciples regarding His death, so He just smiled at Magnus and gave him His permission to do his best.

Magnus Meets with the Disciples

From the police station, Magnus sent a group text to the disciples asking to meet with him the next day at 9:00a.m.

He knew that he needed to tell the group what has happened to Jesus before the news was broken to the public, and as he was driving over, he was rehearsing want he was to say to everyone. As his mind was wondering, he thought about Brayden. Where was he on the night in question? How many countless times in public did people mistake Brayden for Jesus?

With this new possibility of Brayden being the murderer, put Magnus in a different frame of mind. One, that Jesus will be found innocent, and two, how could Brayden deceive them all.

Once settled down amongst his friends, he noticed that Brayden was there. He really thought that he would have some sort of excuse and not show up, but there he was, having the same look of concern as everyone else did in the room.

"Well, my friends," he began, "there is no easy way to say this, but I'm asking you to please listen to everything I need to say and hold all your questions until I finish. Jesus has been arrested for the murder of Jonny." And just as he knew what would happen, no one paid attention to what he had just said about not saying anything until he finished.

The entire room became a flurry of different conversations, hearing, "Not Jesus," "Jesus couldn't hurt anyone," and "There must be a mistake," and Magnus waited patiently until the conversations had ended.

"Here are the facts, my friends," he began, "there was a security camera showing Jonny and somebody who looked like Jesus from a distance. The zoom-in function on the camera is not working, so when the police department found footage from another security camera in the same area, they noticed that there were three witnesses in the area.

To make a long story short, these three witnesses were questioned separately and give the exact same story. They heard Jesus and Jonny arguing about whose ministry is the greatest, and there is room for only one true ministry. We know what the law says about witnesses that we need at least two or three to corroborate any story, in which they did. Of course the police department asked Jesus where He was during the time in question, and unfortunately for Jesus, He was alone praying, as He usually does.

"Before I go any further, Brayden, let me ask you where you were that night?" asked Magnus.

Brayden had the where-with-all to look shocked, as if to say, "You suspect me?"

The Xians took every precaution to have an air-tight alibi for Brayden for the night in question. He had taken selfies with other members of the Xian group from the day before, had someone from their IT group somehow change the date and time to reflect the time and date in questioned. Yes, the devil is into technology!

When Brayden produced the proof of where he was that particular night, sadness again enveloped the room.

As everyone was gathering their things to leave, Magnus half-heartedly told them the conversation he had with Jesus the night before, regarding how He knew this trial would end, and how he told Jesus that he will prove to the world that He was innocent if it was the last thing that he would do!

Everyone hugged as they said their goodbyes.

News About Jesus Being Arrested

"*Jesus Arrested For The Murder Of His Cousin Jonny*"—which was not only the main headline on each and every newspaper in the world, it was also plastered though out the internet. You couldn't open any search engine without this being the topic of discussion.

Once reading this news about Jesus, hope for Jedidiah and Nine went away for a brief second, but they wouldn't let the joy they found once becoming a follower of Jesus Christ interfere with what they read. There must be a mistake.

After being baptized by Jesus, with this new season of hope, they both shared their newfound faith with their families. Both sides of their families also accepted Jesus Christ as their personal savior. It was simple because their family saw the difference in their appearance, the way their eyes lit up when they spoke about Jesus, but also the joy that they had in their spirit when they spoke. Whatever they had, their family wanted to be a part of that.

They wanted to feel close to Jesus during His time in need, and the only way to do that was to make sure they stayed connected to His disciples.

After Jedidiah and Nine were baptized by Jesus, He introduced them to His disciples, and they all felt an immediate connection and made promises to keep in touch. What they both learned from being around Jesus and His disciples was priceless, something you couldn't learn in books or off the internet.

They knew about their normal scheduled meetings and decided to go be with them.

Jesus' Trial

The Xians had a member of their group who was also a judge. They somehow managed to have this specific judge preside over Jesus' trial because they wanted to make sure they could impose the worst possible outcome and to make sure they also humiliate Jesus in the process.

The one thing that they knew they had on their side is what The Book of the Law says about death. If a person kills another person in anger and on purpose, then that person is to also be killed.

Considering this is the first killing in history, the Xians felt they had the upper hand and wanted to take advantage of this situation. Humiliating Jesus and having the worst possible execution would be an example to deter others from committing a murder.

In their own secret meetings, the Xians came up with a plan for Jesus not only to die on a cross but for Him to carry His own cross from the courtroom, where He was being held, to the open field where they had designated the cross would stand.

What a field day the media would have.

The Xians loved having attention, so not only had they made room in the courtroom for the media, they had security cameras mounted on the outside of the structure Roby had quickly built that would house Jesus' body once He died.

Again, the Xians were only thinking about how this authoritative act would make them look in the public's eye.

The word had spread regarding Jesus and how He had told His disciples that He would be raised on the third day after dying, so prior to the trial, being confident on how it would end, having a security camera mounted outside the building where Jesus' body was to be taken when the doors are opened on the third day, and the body was still there, people would know that Jesus lied, and life would go on as it had been before Jonny and Jesus!

The day of the trial arrived, and Magnus was prepared to fight for Jesus.

The largest courtroom that was available was filled to capacity with His mother and family members being on the first row, the second row with His disciples, plus Jedidiah and Nine. The rest of the audience were filled with spectators and those of the media.

The trial itself didn't take that long.

The prosecuting attorney only had his three star witnesses testified to what had happened on the night in question, and as hard as Magnus tried to find any holes in their story, which they had rehearsed time and time again, he couldn't.

He kept looking at the jurors to see if he could read them, to see if they might show any compassion toward Jesus, even though he knew they had to deliberate only on the facts that were presented to them about the crime, not to what they knew in their hearts about Jesus.

Magnus' closing argument regarding Jesus was quite moving, stating facts about who He was, who He represented and the many miracles that occurred during His ministry, had people in tears.

The judge dismissed the jurors for the day, ordering them to use the remaining part of the day to deliberate and come back early the next morning with their verdict.

The Disciples Visit with Jesus

The disciples of Jesus didn't know what to expect when they were asked to come to the place where Jesus was being held while awaiting the verdict.

What they found was Jesus, sitting in a sparsely furnished room that was cold and dark. The only light in the room came from one window and that light shone directly on Jesus.

Jesus had the same look on His face as He did when they were meeting in someone's home, no stress showing whatsoever. A serene, peaceful look that He had was passed on to the souls of His disciples. They might not have understood why they were feeling a sense of peace instead of having the feelings of being angry, nervous, and distraught, but no one fought the feeling. Instead they were happy just to be around Jesus.

Even Brayden showed up because he didn't want to draw any extra attention to himself by not continuing to be a part of the group, even if he wasn't sure how Jesus would act toward him once they saw each other.

Jesus hugged everyone as if they were His best friend, and when He hugged Brayden, He hugged him just a few seconds longer than anyone else, and during that short time, Jesus whispered into Brayden's ear without any malicious tone in His voice, "I forgive you, Brayden."

Hearing these words come out of Jesus' mouth was too much for Brayden to take. He told everyone that he needed to leave right away because he wasn't feeling well, which was not a lie.

Jesus took this priceless opportunity to explain again what His ministry was all about and to remind them that He will see them all again, for them to have faith and hope that He will be lifted up to draw all men to Him.

The disciples had been around Jesus long enough to know that when He had said things, they would not question Him.

The many miracles He performed always had the hope that He spoke about, and because they knew that Magnus was the best attorney around, they expected a miracle for the verdict for the first murder trial in the world.

The Jury Is Back with the Verdict

Once everyone in the courtroom had settled in their seats, the judge entered and asked the jurors had they reached a unanimous decision, to which the foreman replied, "Yes, we have, your honor."

"Please read your verdict," the judge said.

"We the jurors, find Jesus guilty of murdering Jonny!"

At this statement, the crowd erupted in disbelief, wailing, crying uncontrollably, and shouts of 'no's' from those who loved Jesus.

The judge had to bang his gavel on the desk several times to ask for order in his court. "Order in the court!' he shouted, "or I will put all of you out of my courthouse." He was bluffing of course, and because he enjoyed all this attention, he was hoping no one called his bluff.

That seemed to grab everyone's attention, and once the room became quiet, he calmly began the speech he had memorized which he and the other Xians had concocted, ready for this guilty verdict.

The judge stood up for a dramatic effect, looked directly into one of the cameras, and delivered his speech. "Ladies and gentlemen, it is with a heavy heart that I am about to impose a sentence for Jesus. After deliberating what I might say, and I believe I am imposing a fair sentence for Jesus—I'm saying fair because it is my intention to use this trial as an example to anyone else who might be entertaining the idea of murder and hopefully this sentence of Jesus will become a deter for that.

"Our Book of the Law says, 'an eye for an eye.' That being said, I had a wooden cross constructed in the possibility that Jesus was found guilty. Jesus will carry His cross down to the area where it will be planted where the cameras are already set up. But before Jesus is to be placed on the cross, He will be beaten on His back by using a cat-of-nine tails, then being supported by ropes, nails will be hammered in His wrist, His feet resting on a small piece of wood, and will remain there until He dies.

"I know this sounds like a harsh treatment, and because this is the first murder that has ever occurred, I'm hopeful by this display of torture, it will become the last. This execution will take place immediately. Court adjourned!" was the last order that the judge shouted.

If you thought the noise level in the courtroom was bad when the verdict was given, this level of noise was deafening.

Jesus' mother didn't waste any time reaching her Son, and once she reached Him, she wouldn't let Him go until an officer of the court pried her arms off Him. It was at that moment that all of the disciples gathered around His mom to give her their support even if they felt as bad as she did.

As the officers of the court escorted Jesus out of the courtroom to get ready for His execution, the disciples, Jesus' family and friends gathered outside the courtroom with the exception of Magnus and Brayden.

The group held on to one another for support, and someone said, "When we met with Jesus earlier today, He said that He would be lifted high so that He would draw all men to Him, but in my wildest thoughts, did I ever think He meant literally."

A few moments later, Jesus appeared from the side door, dressed in a different outfit, with a few men carrying the cross that Jesus was to carry.

"How is that fair!" Dre' shouted. "It took three of you to carry this cross on a flat surface to Jesus, and you expect one man to carry it by Himself up a hill. That's crazy!" Dre' quickly took it upon himself to give instructions to Jesus' family and friends.

"It's approximately seven miles to where this execution is to take place," started Dre'. "If we get into groups of threes with Jesus walking within our group and walk about a quarter of a mile each, and rotating, we can accomplish this without Jesus carrying His own cross and without us getting tired," Dre' ended.

Everyone agreed this was a great idea. Anything to help Jesus.

As they walked down the streets which was lined up with spectators, Jesus' mom was the only person that held His hand during the entire walk.

Magnus and Brayden's absence was noticed by DJ, Kaylee, and Lincoln. "Where's Magnus and Brayden?" they asked one another.

****

Magnus knew that the answer for Jesus to be found innocent was in the footage of the security camera, so he stayed behind, and instead of going to the execution, he went through the footage again.

Inch by inch, he fast-forwarded the film. Inch by inch, he rewound the film. This went on for some time and still nothing. The zoom-in function was still not working either.

Something in his spirit told him to pray, so he did. "Father God, I should have prayed to You first before trying to accomplish this task on my own. Jesus is always telling us that You care about every aspect of our lives, whether it is a huge problem or something small, You care and want to be a part of it. I'm asking You now Father God to please make the zoom-in function on this security camera work, so that I can prove Jesus' innocence to the world."

The moment he ended the prayer, he heard a small hum in the camera so he knew it was working. What he saw shocked him!

"It's Brayden!" he said, and if that wasn't enough proof, Brayden killed Jonny with his left hand, and Jesus is right-handed.

Magnus didn't waste any time once he said thank You to God for His help in reaching Jesus before His execution.

He looked at his watch, and it was already three in the afternoon, and because the streets were so crowded, he couldn't run. Having the camera, he could only walk fast, weaving in and out of the crowds.

****

During the long walk, someone in the crowd offered Jesus a chair to sit on to let Him take a quick break.

It was during this time He looked up and said to God, "Father God, I know that it took Me awhile to accept My mantle in life, and I thank You for Your patience, grace, and mercy on My life. Father, I know that I was born for a specific reason." He continued on, saying, "My Father, if it is possible, to let this cup of suffering be taken away from Me, yet I want Your will to be done, not Mine."

After which Jesus stood up and walked the last mile to His destination.

With food vendors setting up their booths and music playing, you would have thought a celebration was taking place and not an execution.

It was in the afternoon, and where the sun should have been shining, it was becoming like dusk.

The men who had the responsibility of lifting Jesus onto His cross looked uneasy, knowing what they were ordered and paid to do.

Once they planted the cross in the ground, the height of the cross was approximately fifteen feet and weighed one hundred and fifty pounds, the men used straps supported by a crane to lift Jesus to the cross, but before they lifted Jesus, the Xians hired a person specifically to whip Jesus' back with an old-fashion cat-of-nine tails, more evidence of how they would humiliate Jesus.

As each man's responsibility was to secure an arm and to drive a nail into Jesus' wrist, the young man who was on Jesus' right side, as he held the nail, ready to hammer it into His wrist, took this opportunity to quickly and quietly speak to Jesus. Looking directly into those eyes of compassion, he said to Jesus, "Jesus, I believe that You are the Son of God, and this is just a job for me. I've been following Your ministry and would like to accept You as my personal savior and please forgive me of my sins."

"Son," Jesus said, "your sins have been forgiven."

The young man quickly hammered the nail into Jesus' wrist and came down as quickly as possible. His partner finished before he did.

The sky became darker and darker.

Logan calculated that it would take Jesus approximately six hours to die. Having a fever, loss of blood, and the strain upon His muscles on His chest, he was not wrong.

Six hours later, Jesus cried out in a loud voice, "It is done!" and drew His last breath, at which this exact moment, the earth shook, and in some places, the ground opened.

The Xians wanted to make sure before they took Jesus down that He was dead, so they went to Ezra and asked him what the main source of life in a person's body is. Is it the heart or what?

Ezra explained that the main source of life in a person's body is the blood. Without blood in a person's body, that person cannot live, so they demanded one of the young men, who had previously placed a nail in Jesus' wrist, and told him to go find a sharp object, such as a knife and make a deep hole in Jesus side so He would bleed out.

It didn't matter that the young man didn't have any medical knowledge as to where the best place would be to pierce Jesus. He was more concerned that he would be getting more money for this act.

Once they brought Jesus' body down, both Logan and his brother Ezra sadly confirmed Jesus' death. The death certificate stated, "Hung until death," signed by both brothers.

The structure that Roby had built for Jesus' final resting place was outside the city, so they had arranged for truck to be on call with a mattress in its bed to pick up Jesus' body, and the family, disciples, and friends would meet there.

As they were placing Jesus' body in the truck, Magnus ran over to the truck, saw Jesus' body in the truck, draped his body with the camera over the side of the rail, more for support after seeing Jesus' body than anything before he told everyone what he found.

"Brayden killed Jonny!" he shouted. "The zoom-in function started working, and I was able to see the face of the person that killed Jonny. It was Brayden. Brayden who is also left-handed, and Jesus is right-handed. I don't know why Brayden did it, and I guess he'd be the only one who can tell us," Magnus ended.

The media, who still had their cameras rolling as they were following the disciples around, heard what Magnus had said and they didn't waste any time calling their perspective stations who broke into the regularly scheduled programs with this breaking news.

Magnus kept his word to Jesus by proving to the world He was innocent, and everyone also knew that Brayden was responsible for the murder of Jonny.

This guilt which consumed Brayden caused him to commit suicide as soon as he saw Jesus die on the cross! He neither waited to see if Jesus would arise in three days or spend the money that he received from the Xians.

Along with the entire world who witnessed Jesus' execution, and those who were close to Jesus felt such a huge loss.

Sure, all the disciples went back to work to help keep from feeling that void that they all felt, but what was making everything so much worse was the betrayal of Brayden.

"Why? Why did he do it?" was the question everyone had and was afraid that they would never know the answer because he had killed himself.

Jesus Is Alive

Prior to Jesus being arrested, Jedidiah and Nine had become close to Jesus' mother Marisol, and when she asked them to pick her up on the third day after Jesus' crucifixion so she could anoint her Son's body with spices, they said, "Okay."

During the ride to the tomb, there was the usual polite questions "How are you? How are you feeling?" because no one really felt like talking.

Marisol did feel they deserved an answer to why would she bring spices for her Son, three days after His death and her explanation was simple, "God told me too."

As they walked closer to the building, they all noticed at once that the door, which was locked and only Marisol had the key to, was opened.

They started running toward the building, not knowing what to expect. What they saw was a young man in a white robe, sitting on the right side of the clothes that Jesus had on, folded in a neat pile, but no Jesus.

"Who took Jesus?" all three said at the same time to the young man.

"Did He not tell you that He would rise on the third day?" the young man calmly said. "He is not here, and He sent me to tell you that He will see you and the disciples again very soon."

Afraid of what was happening, the three of them walked back to their car, their bodies trembling as if their legs couldn't hold them up and decided between the three of them, for the time being, they wouldn't say anything to anyone else.

The next morning, Aaliyah, Maya, and Kaylee decided to jog around the area where Jesus was laid.

Once they were close to the building, they saw a man dressed in white, standing nearby, and as they got closer to Him, they saw that it was Jesus! They couldn't believe what they saw!

"Jesus!" they said as they had a group hug.

Jesus told them the same thing the young man told His mother, Jedidiah, and Nine—that He would visit with them soon and for them to go tell the disciples that they had seen Him.

That evening, the disciples had already scheduled a meeting on the same day that Jesus had shown Himself to Aaliyah, Maya, and Kaylee, so it was perfect timing for them to share the news with the others.

"We saw Jesus!" Aaliyah said.

"We all hugged Him!" said Kaylee

"And He said He'll see us soon!" chimed in Maya.

"What are we waiting for?" asked Lincoln. "Let's go see for ourselves if what they are saying is true."

They all piled into their cars and headed over to the site. The conversations in each car centered around Jesus being alive!

"I won't believe it's Jesus until I see the holes in His wrist," said Logan.

"I want to have a one-on-one talk with Him and see what's on His agenda," stated Lincoln, letting his managerial skills kick in, forgetting about everything else Jesus had said.

DJ, being his quiet self, thought what great pictures he could take to share with the world that Jesus is alive.

Even though Ezra knew that Jesus was the Son of God, he thought that he could possible get a DNA sample from Him to see what's different about Him, that could maybe help keep someone else from dying from a disease.

"Let's have a party," Harper said, "and I'll do all the cooking."

It was hard to contain the excitement everyone was feeling to see Jesus again, and once all the cars reached the site, and everyone got out, they all expected to see Jesus meet them there.

What they saw was the same thing Jesus' mother, Jedidiah, and Nine saw. The clothes that He wore, neatly folded up, but no sign of Jesus.

Everyone looked at Kaylee, Maya, and Aaliyah as if to say, "Where is He?"

The only thing the three of them could say is "We don't know why He isn't here."

They all still decided to go over to Harper's house instead of going to their own homes, who promised to feed them "comfort" food to raise their spirits.

Harper immediately went to her kitchen to start cooking while the rest of the group remained in the living room, sitting around not speaking to one another.

When the tension in the room couldn't seem to get any thicker, Jesus appeared in the middle of the room!

Once the shock wore off, and the group realized they weren't imagining seeing Jesus, they all gathered around Him to give Him a hug.

Jesus' body was no longer flesh but a spiritual body, and although He just appeared in the middle of the room, His body seemed to be like everyone else's.

Harper stopped what she was doing when she heard the commotion in the living room, thinking that everyone was just hungry. Being a chef, she took with her the platter of appetizers that she always had in her freezer, ready in case of unexpected company, and almost dropped the platter when she saw Jesus.

Jesus smiled at Harper as He took one of the appetizers off the platter and ate it! "Delicious as usual, Harper," said Jesus, which made Harper smile.

Once the group calmed down enough to let Jesus speak, He wanted to put everyone's doubting to rest, which included Logan.

"My friends," He started, "while I was still with you, I tried to prepare you for My death. I'm here now to not only show you My scars but to impart the Holy Spirit upon you."

He turned both of His hands palms up so the disciples could see the holes in His wrists where the nails had been hammered, raised His shirt to show the stripes on His back and His side where it was beaten and pierced. Only a few of the them were bold enough to touch the places where Jesus was wounded.

Jesus' resurrection confirmed to everyone that He was the Son of God, also appearing to people to allow them to see and touch Him.

As Jesus gathered His disciples around Himself, He said, "Peace be with you! As the Father has sent Me, I am sending you." And with that, He breathed on them and said, "Receive the Holy Spirit."

By Jesus imparting the Holy Spirit to His disciples, He was preparing them to go into the world as witnesses in the wisdom and power of the Holy Spirit, and at this same time, Jesus reminded them again that now that they have received the Holy Spirit, they can go do greater works that He did.

Not having God's divine power and the Holy Spirit's presence within them, there was no hope of succeeding to keep Jesus' ministry alive by spreading the good news!

Jesus' goal was to complete His mission of redemption that would be accomplished by His death and resurrection. Jesus came to earth to die for sins of the world.

Jesus' message to the disciples was simple. Talk about salvation, having a personal relationship with Jesus. Do not let His death mean nothing. The stripes on His back, the blood that was spilled—these represent the healing. The promises, by believing on His name and that there is power in the name of Jesus and His death on the cross, represents that.

Go throughout the world, preaching, teaching, and healing and even bringing back the dead to life.

Jesus stayed on the earth around forty more days to demonstrate to His followers that He truly was alive and to also teach His disciples and prepare them for the task of telling the world about Christ.

Xians Reactions After
the Resurrection

The group was hot with angry to say the least!

Not only did their plan backfire with Jesus' execution being televised once the stories about Him being seen by others began circulating proved that He was the Son of God, the world saw with their own eyes how He was tortured, whipped and finally being pierced in His side. They also saw how both Ezra and Logan examined Jesus' body and confirmed that He was dead.

How would they spin this story to their benefit?

"Has anyone checked on the security camera outside of the structure where His body was kept?" someone asked.

"Yes," said the judge who had presided over Jesus' trial. He continued saying, "That was the first thing that I did when I heard the stories circulating about Jesus being seen, and I'm telling you that there was no human movement whatsoever during those three days after the execution, however, I did destroy the tapes from the security camera, and we can start a rumor that Jesus' body was stolen and eventually the talk about Jesus being seen alive will die down."

After some time had passed, not only were there more followers of Christ, Jahi had gone missing.

A Year Later

For the gospel to be spread, the disciples went their separate ways to preach about the good news, and because Jesus' death was televised, plus the news the He was alive had also traveled, people were both willing and curious to hear what the disciples had to say.

The disciples used their teachings from Jesus plus their love for people to draw large crowds to hear about salvation and accepting Jesus Christ as their personal savior.

There was a website that Jonny had created to track the number of people who had accepted Jesus as their personal savior, and for logistic reasons, also the city in which they lived.

During the time that both Jonny and Jesus was alive, the number increased at a steady pace.

Once Jesus had died, and Magnus had proved to the world that He was innocent, the numbers on the website increased by 50 percent and once the news of Jesus being alive had spread, it increased to over 100 percent and at times the website was so busy, you couldn't log on and had to come back at a later time.

Not only did these statistics encourage the disciples but also encouraged others to be disciples as well. The churches around the world were not only seeing a greater number of people attending church but accepting Jesus Christ as their personal savior.

For Jedidiah and Nine, this was a new season for their relationship. They both wanted the same thing, marriage and a family, but something kept both their attention from getting to that point.

Neither one of them wouldn't or couldn't let go what had happened to Brayden at the end, only because they had spent so much time with the disciples that everyone was like a brother or a sister to them. His act of suicide was personal to them so they made a decision to put their creative brains together again to solve this missing piece of the puzzle, not fully realizing what deep, dark mysteries was awaiting them as they began their next quest as they put their personal lives on hold and possible in danger.

About the Author

P at currently lives in Anaheim, California with her husband of thirty-three years. She is the mother of four sons, daughters-in-love, and at the time of publishing this book, she is "Nana" to eleven amazing grandkids.

She loves both encouraging and talking to people, so it's no wonder she can be found serving at the information center at her church, The Rock in Anaheim, California, which she loves.

Pat wrote this book primarily to show the world that God is a god who loves us unconditionally, who wants to have a relationship with each and every one of us no matter what our past may have looked like, and also to use her imagination to the "what ifs" to create a world of utopia.